"What do you like in a man, Elizabeth?"

She looked at Cole for a long moment, then tilted her face up to his in silent invitation. "Surprises."

It was as if she was pulling him in. He'd always been an immovable object, someone who couldn't be swayed toward a path if he didn't want to be. But maybe he did want to be swayed, did want to be persuaded. All he knew was that he didn't have the ironclad control over his mind and body he'd had for as far back as he could remember.

It disturbed the hell out of him. But it didn't stop him from slipping his fingers into her hair.

He felt the pull intensify, but he didn't fight it. He wasn't sure he could have even if he'd wanted to.

And he *didn't* want to.

Dear Reader,

The weather's hot, and so are all six of this month's Silhouette Intimate Moments books. We have a real focus on miniseries this time around, starting with the last in Ruth Langan's DEVIL'S COVE quartet, *Retribution.* Mix a hero looking to heal his battered soul, a heroine who gives him a reason to smile again and a whole lot of danger, and you've got a recipe for irresistible reading.

Linda Turner's back—after *way* too long—with the first of her new miniseries, TURNING POINTS. A beautiful photographer who caught the wrong person in her lens has no choice but to ask the cops—make that *one particular cop*—for help, and now both her life and her heart are in danger of being lost. FAMILY SECRETS: THE NEXT GENERATION continues with Marie Ferrarella's *Immovable Objects,* featuring a heroine who walks the line between legal, illegal—and love. *Dangerous Deception* from Kylie Brant continues THE TREMAINE TRADITION of mixing suspense and romance—not to mention sensuality— in doses no reader will want to resist. And don't miss our stand- alone titles, either. Cindy Dees introduces you to *A Gentleman and A Soldier* in a military reunion romance that will have your heart pounding and your fingers turning the pages as fast as they can. Finally, welcome Mary Buckham, whose debut novel, *The Makeover Mission,* takes a plain Jane and turns her into a princess—literally. Problem is, this princess is in danger, and now so is Jane.

Enjoy them all—and come back next month for the best in romantic excitement, only from Silhouette Intimate Moments.

Yours,

Leslie J. Wainger
Executive Editor

Please address questions and book requests to:
Silhouette Reader Service
U.S.: 3010 Walden Ave., P.O. Box 1325, Buffalo, NY 14269
Canadian: P.O. Box 609, Fort Erie, Ont. L2A 5X3

MARIE FERRARELLA

Immovable Objects

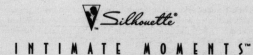

Silhouette®

INTIMATE MOMENTS™

Published by Silhouette Books

America's Publisher of Contemporary Romance

To Susan Litman,
who has to put it all together

Special thanks and acknowledgment are given to
Marie Ferrarella for her contribution to the
FAMILY SECRETS: THE NEXT GENERATION series.

 SILHOUETTE BOOKS

ISBN 0-373-27375-4

IMMOVABLE OBJECTS

Copyright © 2004 by Harlequin Books S.A.

Visit Silhouette Books at www.eHarlequin.com

Printed in U.S.A.

Books by Marie Ferrarella in Miniseries

MARIE FERRARELLA

This RITA® Award-winning author has written over one hundred and twenty books for Silhouette, some under the name Marie Nicole. Her romances are beloved by fans worldwide.

FAMILY SECRETS: THE NEXT GENERATION

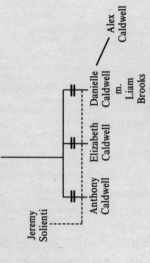

Henry Bloomfield (d.) ~ Deanna Payne

Jeremy Solienti

Anthony Caldwell

Elizabeth Caldwell

Danielle Caldwell
m.
Liam Brooks

Alex Caldwell

Key:
——— Birth Family
– – – Adoptive Family
m. Married
d. Deceased
═══ Triplets

Prologue

The man known simply as Titan to his enemies, head of the mysterious Titan Syndicate, was very aware of his surroundings as he walked the dusky, mean streets of Philadelphia.

This was not the Philadelphia of the Founding Fathers. It was raw and edgy and dangerous. Still, a rare note of fondness vibrated within him. He'd preferred Chicago, but even Philly was better than being exiled in Europe.

Europe had not been to his liking. But staying there had been necessary. Otherwise, all he would have seen of his native country would have been the inside of a jail cell.

Because small minds didn't understand.

The FBI had been breathing down his neck then.

But now the tables were turned and he was a problem for them, not the other way around. He enjoyed taunting, being one step ahead. He'd even taken to sending enigmatic postcards to that dolt Agent Liam Brooks. It excited him to be the thorn in that idiot's side.

Peasants, all of them, stupid Neanderthal peasants with their insignificant lives, their annoying laws and their narrow way of seeing things. Didn't they realize that he was a genius? A genius who saw potential for power, for greatness, while others sleepwalked through their humdrum existences, paying attention to confining things like right and wrong. Allowing that narrow view to get in the way of progress.

Yes, he did enjoy leading them around by their noses, these tin demigods with their code of ethics and their long arms. Just because that stupid New York senator had overdosed on the drug. *His* drug. The "honorable" senator had been an unwitting guinea pig, a step closer to the right direction.

But the drug wasn't quite ready yet.

And the FBI was looking for him, or someone like him.

The anal fools had blown up his lab in Chicago, killing some of his people. People were replaceable, time was not. They were preventing him from perfecting the drug that would ultimately allow him to control key people. Allow him to be a puppet master until he was ready to take center stage, where he rightfully belonged.

But that day was still on the horizon. Right now, in order to complete his experiments, reach the right kind of chemical balance, he needed more information. More key input.

And he needed to find those brats again, all six of them.

Even if he had to move heaven and earth and destroy all the angels in the process to do it, he would reach his goal. He was born to be a leader. It was his due, his right.

It wasn't by chance that he'd selected for himself the name of Titan.

Chapter 1

"Missing? What do you mean it's missing?"

The resonant voice bounced around the sleek, four-hundred-square-foot office on the top floor of the Williams Media Building. Not a man easily ruffled, Cole Williams found himself on his way to furious over this unexpected little bomb that had just been dropped in his lap.

These kinds of things did not just "happen," they were orchestrated.

Ice-blue eyes, known to freeze people far braver than Jack Dobson, narrowed as Cole looked at the man who had come into his domain bearing the news. "A priceless statue doesn't just walk away on its own."

"No, sir, it doesn't, but when we opened the crate it was supposed to be in—it wasn't there." His oversize Adam's apple bobbed up and down like a cork that refused to be sunk. "Mr. Hagen doesn't know what to make of it. He's looking into it right now." Dobson's voice cracked.

Taylor Hagen was the chief investigator kept on retainer by Cole. He had witnessed the statue being crated and then followed the van transporting it.

Terrific, Cole thought.

His new art gallery opening was in a week and Rodin's statue, *Venus Smiling,* the artist's tribute to his beloved late sister, Marie, was to be the center-piece of the entire exhibit. Recognized as the artist's first work and lost for thirty years amid the chaos of western Europe following World War II, it had found its way into billionaire Jonathan MacFarland's private collection. After much negotiating, Cole had managed to secure the twenty-four-inch piece, but only for a little more than a week. Nine days to be exact. A sizable donation was being sent to one of Mac-Farland's favorite charities in exchange for the show-ing. It was the first time the statue was to have seen the light of public day since MacFarland had acquired it fifteen years ago, and it promised to attract an even greater crowd than had originally been anticipated.

Because of his self-made stature and his ability to turn almost anything he touched to gold, Cole Wil-liams, tall, blond and good-looking in a publicity agent's dream sort of way, was the darling of both the business and the celebrity world.

His position was made that much more unique be-cause of his strong ethical beliefs. He'd gotten to where he was today with no backstabbing, no character assassination. He always ran a clean campaign, fought a clean fight. Not an easy feat in the world of media or publishing, and Cole had a well-entrenched foot in both.

But clean rubbed some people the wrong way. There were those who would have liked nothing better than to see him fall from grace, and if they had to create the scenario in order to accommodate the situation, so be it.

Someone had it in for him. Trouble was, because of the businesses he was in, the list of potential character assassins was far from short.

But he didn't have time to wonder who had done this to him. Right now, what was necessary was implementing damage control. And fast.

Cole frowned. Dobson was still standing in his office, still shaking without giving any signs of stopping.

"Get a grip, man, I'm not going to eat you," Cole snapped. "Anything else missing?"

Dobson moved his head from side to side like a deranged windshield wiper. "No, sir, just the statue. We checked. All the other paintings are still there."

Thank God for small favors. Cole picked up the phone receiver. "What about the surveillance tape?"

He had a feeling he knew the answer to that one, but there was no harm in asking. Sometimes, the best of thieves made stupid mistakes. And whoever had taken this statue had just made a colossal one.

Wide, watery eyes watched Cole's every move. "The system's down, sir."

So much for luck and stupid mistakes. "Get it back up and running."

Dobson looked relieved to offer a piece of positive information. "Already working on that, sir."

"Good."

Cole waved the man out. His mind was already on the next step. Being able to quickly anticipate all sides of a problem was what had brought him to the place he now occupied in the world.

That and a wide network of friends and acquaintances he knew he could rely on for their skills and discretion.

There was only one man he knew of who could handle the problem he was facing.

Lorenzo Manelli.

He didn't keep the man's number on speed dial, but it was a number he'd committed to memory long ago. Manelli's talents were unique, as was his price. But there was none better. And he needed Lorenzo now.

Despite the calm facade he projected, Cole could feel the tension rising within him as he waited for the ringing on the other end to cease and for an unrecorded voice to come on.

When he heard a heavily accented voice murmur a greeting, Cole breathed a silent sigh of relief.

"Lorenzo, I have a job that requires your special talents."

A soft, distant chuckle told him he need have no

further concern. Whatever the request, it would be handled.

And then a melodic voice instructed, "Go ahead."

She'd never been alone before.

In her thirty-one years, Elizabeth Caldwell had never really been on her own, never walked into an apartment, closed the door and just taken in the silence, knowing that if she didn't do anything to change it herself, the circumstances would remain this way.

She'd be alone.

Without Anthony. Without Danielle.

Of course, there was still Jeremy Solienti, the man she thought of as Fagin to her Oliver. *Their* Oliver, she amended, because whatever had concerned her had also concerned Anthony and Danielle, and they were all connected in ways that went beyond the normal connections experienced by triplets. It was as if, psychically, there was an open telephone line that connected the three of them, night and day, to one another.

Except that Danielle had chosen to hang up.

First Danielle and now her. Or Anthony, depending on which side of the heated argument you looked at. And it had been a doozy, she thought, kicking off her shoes and sinking onto the newly purchased sofa bed that took up residence in the middle of the room.

Danielle had opted to strike out on her own years ago, to leave the world of con games, teetering on the brink of falling over the invisible line that separated the right side of the law from the wrong. Jeremy, their once unofficial guardian, now employer and eternal mentor, made sure that the jobs they hired out to do always kept them a hairbreadth within the law, even if some of the methods they used in getting the jobs done could certainly not stand up to close scrutiny.

But then, laws had not been passed to accommodate those who had been ''blessed,'' she thought with an enigmatic smile. She reached for the remote to turn on the television set, then decided against it.

Decided to absorb the silence a little longer.

In her case, the blessing had come in the guise of telekinetic powers that allowed her, when she concentrated very hard, to move small objects and make them do her bidding. When she and Dani and Anthony combined their powers, there was nothing they couldn't do. For a price. The price went to line Jeremy's coffers.

Not that the man, in his own way, wasn't good to them. In a move that made life stranger than fiction, Jeremy Solienti, a one-time mercenary, had wound up being their salvation. They were runaways on the verge of getting into serious trouble when he'd come across them. On the street with no money, they'd been reduced to becoming common pickpockets. Dani had picked Jeremy's pocket at a carnival and the man had chased after her, finally cornering all of them as they attempted to flee.

Once he'd taken back what was his, he quickly assessed the situation. Childless, with a soft spot for kids and an eye out for talent, he'd offered them a home. His.

They'd been leery of him, but because they had nowhere else to go, they'd looked at one another and silently agreed.

Jeremy had been sharp enough to pick up on their unique ability to communicate with each other. And their other abilities as well, as time went on. Comfortably wealthy with a vast network of informants and people who owed him favors, Jeremy set about incorporating the latest addition to his little "family." He saw to it that they got a good education, both academic and otherwise.

Because of Jeremy, they didn't become just more statistics in an endless stream of runaways. They could pass themselves off as anything they wanted to with ease and poise. And in exchange for food, shelter and education, Jeremy availed himself of their unique powers, turning them into a new kind of team.

Her mouth curved in a smile. She supposed what they eventually became was something akin to the X-Men meet the A-Team. Granted, they didn't have superpowers, but they were definitely not the average person on the street, either. Because the average person on the street couldn't move objects with his or her mind, couldn't control things without lifting a finger or connect to other human beings and hear their thoughts.

The latter was a connection she had with Anthony and Dani, or rather had had, until Dani had gone "offline," so to speak.

But then a couple of weeks ago, Dani had come "on-line" again. Out of the blue, her sister had touched her thoughts because she needed help. She wanted her to promise to take care of her son, Alex, if anything ever happened to her.

She'd told Anthony about it. And then all hell had broken loose.

The confrontation had taken place in their apartment, the one that Anthony insisted they share so that he could "look after her."

"Look, she walked out on us, we didn't walk out on her," he'd railed, furious, when she tried to get him to talk about Dani. To mend broken fences so that they could be a family again.

Elizabeth tried very hard not to take his outburst personally, not to let his yelling affect her. She knew better than anyone how Anthony felt about things, how sensitive he actually was. When Danielle had left them abruptly to go off on her own, their brother had taken it as a sign of abandonment. Another in a long line of abandonments, beginning with their mother.

Of course, that hadn't exactly been of their mother's own volition. Deanna Payne had been killed when they were only three, strangled in their living room. When the commotion had begun that awful, sticky summer night, Anthony had shoved both Elizabeth and Danielle into the closet to keep them safe. He'd stayed with them, telling them to be quiet as the clothes around them cocooned the sounds of raised voices and then the screams.

And then there was silence, an awful silence that

ate into the darkness. Anthony slipped out first, telling them to stay where they were.

She'd stayed there as long as she could. Until she couldn't anymore. When she ventured out, holding Dani's hand in hers, she saw her brother kneeling on the floor beside the lifeless body of their mother. Her beautiful face was bruised, beaten. And there was blood, so vividly red against her pale, pale lips.

Her little heart hammering, unable to take in the full meaning of what she saw, she'd knelt on one side of her mother while Dani had knelt on the other. They'd each taken one of their mother's hands and tried to will her back to life.

She wasn't sure when her brother had gotten up to call the police, but she knew he had. Just as, somewhere in her heart, she knew that it had been their father who had killed their mother.

But Anthony had never confirmed it, never said yes or no when she asked. It was a piece of himself he'd kept locked away from both her and Dani. The police took him at his word when he'd told them he didn't know who had done this. People didn't waste too much time questioning a three-year-old.

Whether or not their father had killed their mother, Benedict Payne had disappeared from their lives that night. It was the second abandonment.

The foster system they found themselves catapulted into was fraught with abandonments. They were yanked from one home to another, sometimes taken in all together, sometimes taken in separately.

Throughout it all, they'd managed to maintain their silent connection.

Until now.

Dani had used a conventional method, the telephone, to connect with her, calling her several days ago to reconnect. Her sister had called to tell her things Dani felt she needed to know. Unique though they thought themselves to be, they were far from alone. That there were others like them, others with ''gifts'' that did not belong to ordinary people. In addition, the DNA test results which Danielle had undergone to prove the link and which had involved samples from each of the fellow ''gifted'' individuals were now unaccounted for at the private lab where they had been processed and stored. It wasn't a case of misplacement, but something more. Something, Dani confided, far more sinister.

It had been a great deal to assimilate and Elizabeth wasn't a hundred percent sure she believed all of it, even though she knew that Dani did.

Elizabeth pressed her lips together. She had no idea if Anthony believed any of it. He'd been too busy yelling at her the last time she'd seen him to discuss it.

They'd just finished up a job, and instead of going out to celebrate, Anthony had insisted they come back home and turn in early in preparation for the next assignment. She remembered being resentful that Anthony constantly controlled her life.

When she'd told him about Dani's call, he'd turned

on her, livid. "Don't you understand? I don't want to hear anything about Dani."

She couldn't make herself believe that he meant what he said. "Anthony, please, just listen—"

His green eyes had darkened. "No, you just listen. Dani made her choice. She left us. Fine, she's gone. We're here and we have a job to do. Now go to bed, we've got an early day tomorrow."

It was then that she'd decided enough was enough. Looking back, she realized she should have taken a stand a long time ago, before Anthony had become so accustomed to controlling her life. "No."

He'd looked at her, astonished, angrier than she'd ever seen him. "What do you mean, 'no'?"

She'd turned her back on him, heading for the front door. Beyond that, she had no clue where she was going.

"It's a two-letter word," she'd said over her shoulder. "You figure it out."

Anthony had grabbed her arm and spun her around to face him. "What's gotten into you?"

And then the dam broke inside her. "What's gotten into me is that I don't want to live this way anymore. I don't want to go from job to job, jumping when you say jump."

Anthony looked as if he didn't know what she was talking about. "Hey, Jeremy is the one who gives the assignments—"

She'd gritted her teeth together, refusing to cave in the way she always did. Her position may have been peacemaker in the family, but that didn't mean she wasn't above making a little war herself. "And you're the one who acts as gatekeeper."

"Gatekeeper?"

"Yes, gatekeeper. To my prison. Anthony, we don't do anything but the jobs that Jeremy gives us. We don't socialize, we don't go out. Just because we have these—these gifts doesn't mean we have to hide like freaks." More than anything, she desperately wanted to spread her wings and fly.

"We're not hiding."

"Well, you certainly try to hide me." One word was leading to another and she couldn't seem to stop. "When have I had a single relationship? You won't let me out of your sight."

"We don't have time for relationships."

"That's just my point. It's always what *you* think is best. There's never any discussion, never any room for another opinion, just yours." His expression had remained impassive. Stony. She might as well have been making her case to a wall. "Damn it, that's why Dani left. You were suffocating her. She wanted to be her own person."

"Fine," he'd shouted. "She has what she wants. She's her own person."

"But that doesn't mean cutting her off, dead."

His eyes were cold, steely. "Can't have it both ways, Lizzie."

Suddenly, the argument was back in her court. It wasn't Dani they were arguing about but her again. And she was fighting for her life. "Why? Why can't I have it both ways? Why can't I work for Jeremy, be your sister and still have a life of my own? Why can't Dani have a life of her own?''

For a moment, there had been genuine concern in his eyes before the wall went up again. ''Because it doesn't work that way. Because we're different. Because things can hurt you out there.''

''I'm thirty-one years old, Anthony. You can't keep me in bubble wrap forever.''

And then he'd taken the ball out of her court. In typical Anthony fashion, he'd made the decision for her, even though he probably hadn't realized it at the time. ''You want to be free? Fine, be free. Go off on your own, just leave me the hell alone.'' The words echoed in his wake as he slammed the door behind him, storming out of their apartment.

At the time, she'd been incensed—and hurt. She ran about, collecting her things and tossing them into the suitcase they used when they went out of town on jobs.

And all the while, she'd filled the spaces in her head with snippets of songs she knew. So that Anthony couldn't tune in and discover what she was up to.

The wheels had been set in motion. She needed her space.

She'd left.

Once inside her car, she placed a call to Jeremy on her cell phone. To say he was surprised when she told him she was going on a much needed vacation was an understatement, especially since she said she was going alone. She'd lied and added she wasn't taking her cell along.

"How can I get in contact with you?" he'd wanted to know.

"I'll call you," she'd promised.

But she hadn't. And she wasn't going to. Not for a while.

When she'd finally let her guard down, she'd discovered that there were no communal thoughts for her to let in. No feeling that something that Anthony was experiencing was touching her.

Like smoke on the wind, Anthony was gone, out of her life, as if he'd never been there.

It felt wonderful to be normal, to be alone with her thoughts.

Wonderful and strange and lonely, she slowly discovered.

So this was what everyone else experienced. After being part of a trio and then a duo for so long, she wasn't all that sure she liked this change completely.

No, she silently argued with herself as the temptation to call Anthony one more time rose within her. Anthony's terms were total surrender.

She sank back against a pillow. It was high time she took the training wheels off her life and rode on her own. Maybe not in a straight line, but at least unassisted.

The apartment she'd gotten was a studio. She had enough money in her account—Jeremy had always been generous with their cut—to get any sort of living accommodations, but she wanted to start out small and see how she liked it.

There was always time to get something bigger later. But she wanted to take baby steps because baby steps guaranteed that you didn't fall flat on your face the way you might if you leaped.

Her attention drifted toward the newspaper she'd picked up earlier. She noticed a large, splashy article about the grand opening of Cole Williams's new gallery. It promised to be a major event with a great many celebrities there, rubbing elbows with the CEOs of industry.

She smiled.

Just the kind of stomping grounds a newly released sparrow was looking for, she thought.

Beside the article was a rendition of the invitation that had been sent out to legions of people who periodically made the news. The article said that the party was "by invitation only."

Her smile grew wider as she reached for a sketch pad. "Not a problem."

Chapter 2

Elizabeth didn't have to glance in the mirror. She knew. Knew that she was a certified, pull-out-all-the-stops knockout.

But a languid review of the evidence certainly didn't hurt.

A smile curved her generous mouth as she looked at her reflection in the freestanding oval mirror that allowed her to get an overall view of herself. Satisfaction wrapped itself around her like a warm, velvety blanket as she surveyed her image.

She was loaded for bear and ready to go.

Rather than some prim hairstyle, she wore her hair loose. Coming down just past her shoulders, the midnight-black torrent of swirls and waves seductively brushed against her bare back. Her eye makeup, done to perfection, brought out her hazel-green eyes and accentuated the Gypsy blood that ran through her veins, thanks to her Romanian mother.

But it was the dress that pulled everything together. A flaming-red bit of fabric that nipped in at her small waist, highlighted her subtly rounded hips and, because the hem flirted outrageously with her thighs, allowed anyone with eyes to take in the fact that she had long, shapely legs that seemed to go on forever.

If this didn't bring the great and near-great mon-eyed men milling around at the gallery opening to their collective knees, then nothing would, she thought with a toss of her head.

Upon scrutiny, Elizabeth couldn't have been ac-cused of having a vain bone in her body, but what she did possess was confidence: confidence in her skills, in her abilities to use them. She knew exactly what to do to stir up a reaction, be it from a crowd or an audience of one.

It didn't take any of her special gifts to bring her to this conclusion; it was instinct, pure and simple. Survival instinct, because once upon a time those same skills had been what had helped her, Anthony and Dani survive on the street after they had run away from their last foster home.

Even after all this time, the memory still sent a shiver sliding down her spine. Living in that house had been surreal. On the outside, they all appeared to be the perfect family, being trotted out to church every Sunday, looking like a Norman Rockwell paint-ing come to life. But once behind closed doors, it had been different, completely different.

Amanda Toliver had been little more than a mousy servant to her husband, Wayne. And Wayne, with his large, beaming smile and his even larger hands, had felt that he was entitled to do whatever he wanted within his own residence.

That had included enforcing his will on the three of them.

Taking a hairbrush from the bureau, Elizabeth ran it through her hair one final time. Toliver had been roughest on Anthony, demanding all sorts of things from him, never satisfied with anything Anthony did. She remembered being surprised that Anthony had taken being ordered around for as long as he had, but she'd been aware of her brother making an effort, a really big effort this time, to blend in. They'd wanted so much to fit in, to have a normal life after what they'd gone through, after all the homes they'd been sent to.

But then it got uglier.

Always smiling at her and her sister, Wayne was constantly reaching out and touching them, petting them, hugging them. They were thirteen and just beginning to mature, but they both felt uncomfortable with what he was doing, even though they tried to reassure each other that it was just harmless.

And then they were forced to face the truth. One night Wayne slipped into their room, the one that she and Dani shared. Sensing someone's presence, she woke up and screamed. Wayne was in her bed.

Anthony came flying in from the next room, his beloved baseball bat in his hand. He swung it against

Wayne, knocking him out. She was sure that Anthony had killed the man. Amanda never came into the room. It was as if she didn't want to know what was happening.

Grabbing their clothes, the three of them fled into the night. To hide from the system. To hide from a society that looked the other way when they were being herded around like so much chattel.

For the next few days, they stole newspapers from people's front steps to find out if there was any mention of Wayne. If Anthony had killed him, there would have been a story, an article, a line. But there wasn't. Wayne Toliver obviously hadn't been killed and the law wasn't looking for Anthony for murder.

It was a relief.

It was also a position they were determined never to put themselves in again. So they stayed hidden, living by their wits and talents. Outcasts again.

On the outside, looking in, that was how they always felt. Even after Jeremy came into their lives and took them in.

The feeling had only intensified because Jeremy found ways for them to make use of their unique talents, talents that set them apart from the rest of the world. A client coming to Jeremy for "help" could be assured that if he'd had something stolen, it would be returned, no matter where it was or how well guarded.

That laws had to be bent in order to retrieve stolen items was something no one concerned themselves about. "Don't ask, don't tell" was an active motto in all of their lives. Jeremy told them more than once that he didn't care how they did something, as long as they covered their trail and that it didn't lead back to them. Or him.

Elizabeth had used some of her personal talents to ensure that she'd gain entrance to the gallery tonight.

The invitation sitting inside her purse on the coffee table had not arrived via mail but via her rather uncanny ability to copy whatever she saw, whether it was a work of art or an invitation to an exclusive gala.

Right now, the latter promised to be more fun.

Elizabeth set the brush down and did a slow turn before the mirror, watching her hair move. She was really looking forward to tonight. Not just because she'd be crashing a gala where the rich were rubbing elbows with one another, but because she truly loved art. In whatever spare time she had away from her duties for Jeremy, she liked to haunt art galleries and museums.

Anthony had no patience with that sort of thing, and even Dani, when she'd been around, had no interest in spending her time staring at sweeping lines and trying to discern different brush strokes, so it had been the one thing she could do on her own.

Elizabeth had gone into her hobby the way she went into everything—wholeheartedly. She'd immersed herself in every single aspect and detail of art.

Her skills ran to forgery. She was able to copy adeptly any style, any artist.

She'd used both skills in printing up her invitation. The rest had required a little research. She'd gotten a lead on the company that had printed the original invitations. Paying a visit to the store, she'd affected a Southern accent and gushed, professing utter admiration for the look of the invitation when it had arrived at her home. The printer had been in the palm of her hand within two minutes, answering her questions unconditionally. After all, what was the harm in telling someone about the kind of paper that was used to print the invitation?

Armed with that and the newspaper photograph of the invitation, the rest was easy.

She smiled to herself as she slipped her wrap around her shoulders and gave herself one last look before picking up her purse. Ready.

Cole had no idea who she was. Only that he quite possibly—despite his wide circle of friends, acquaintances and business associates—had never seen a woman quite this beautiful in his life. In the crowded gallery, he'd noticed her the moment she'd walked into the room.

Taken possession of the room was a more apt description.

He could feel his gut tightening just looking at her, and that kind of thing just didn't happen to him. It had never happened to him, in fact, not even his first time with a woman. And these days, well, women had proven a far too accessible commodity for him to feel anything but the mildest form of fleeting excitement.

He was blessed with good looks on top of his vast fortune, and all he had to do was crook his finger and women fell at his feet, ready and willing. There was no challenge for him. The outcome was always a foregone conclusion. The only eagerness in any physical encounter was displayed on the part of the women he encountered, women who wanted nothing more than to be part of the social whirl he always moved in.

But this one, he could see even at this distance, had a fire in her eyes. The way she moved through the throng, displaying the most self-assured manner he'd ever seen, created a wrinkle in his concentration. Outside of himself, he couldn't recall ever seeing anyone look quite so confident.

And why shouldn't she be confident? When you were drop-dead gorgeous, a certain kind of smugness had to enter into it.

Who the hell was she? And who had invited her? He knew she couldn't be on the list his secretary had him initial. He knew everyone on that list by sight, if not immediately by name.

A possessive squeeze rendered on his forearm brought Cole back to his immediate circumstances. There was a blonde hanging off his arm and apparently on his every word.

Except that he'd stopped talking.

"If you'll excuse me," he began as he ably disengaged himself from the nubile blonde in the almost-dress that kept threatening to slip off her supple body. The woman—Ellen was it?—had hung herself on his arm some fifteen minutes ago, dangling there like an expensive bracelet.

One look at the pout on her face told him that Ellen was not about to go quietly into that good night.

"But I was hoping you could show me your private collection later," she breathed suggestively. Her surgically perfect breasts all but put in a personal appearance, thanks to the filmy white material that was doing an inadequate job of covering them.

Very deliberately, Cole moved out of range. "Perhaps some other time," he said over his shoulder. He'd forgotten about her before the words ever reached the woman's ears.

His mind was elsewhere.

The woman with the killer body and the Gypsy face had just moved toward the centerpiece of the gala, the bronze statue of *Venus Smiling*.

From her expression, the lady in red seemed oblivious to the sensation she was creating in her wake.

Bathed in cool blue lights that shone on it from three directions, *Venus Smiling* was hauntingly exquisite. Almost as exquisite as the woman looking at it, Cole couldn't help thinking.

Approaching her, Cole paused for a moment to spare a glance at the so-called work of art. The work of art that almost wasn't.

You are truly a master, Lorenzo. I have to give you that.

He made a mental note to send the man a gift of appreciation over and above the sum they had agreed on once this whole affair was over. Once he managed to lay his hands on the original and return it, he might even keep Lorenzo's work of art as a souvenir.

As to finding out who had the original, the clock was definitely ticking. Come morning, he was going to have to turn his considerable energies to finding out just what had happened to it. For the last week, his attention had been focused on manipulating the press so that their attention was on the gala, not the piece, until it was ready.

It had been touch and go for a while. At one point, it looked as if he was going to have to postpone the opening, but then Lorenzo had come through, the way he always did. The copy was ready a full eighteen hours before the big opening.

Just enough time for the work to "cool."

Cole had had his doubts, up until the unveiling, that they could pull it off. But when Lorenzo had placed the statue before him, undraping it with a flourish, he'd been speechless. He was by no means an expert, but he certainly couldn't tell the difference between the statue he had been shown in MacFarland's mansion and the one that was now taking its place. Provided with a multitude of photographs, Lorenzo had managed to nail the statue right down to the minute details.

The hunt for the missing statue was for tomorrow. Tonight Cole wanted to enjoy the fruits of his efforts. And possibly to enjoy this young woman who was looking at the sculpture with such rapt attention.

As he came up behind her, he caught a whiff of something seductive that went straight to his gut. That was twice now, he thought.

"It is beautiful, isn't it?"

Elizabeth didn't turn immediately to look at the man standing behind her. Her attention was completely focused on the statue, to the exclusion of everything and everyone else. Situated the way it was, on a tall pedestal within a ring of blue lights and roped off from general access, it was too far away for her to study in detail.

Even so, there was something that bothered her about the statue, something not quite right that she couldn't put her finger on.

Granted she'd only seen the statue once, and that had been on an old VHS tape that dealt with unique pieces of art that had found their way into private collections. But still, there was something nagging her about the statue. She needed a closer look, but she knew hopping over the golden ropes that surrounded the piece would be frowned upon.

"Yes, it is beautiful," she murmured, finally looking away and at the person who addressed her.

Space within the gallery was at a premium. Rubbing elbows was not only a euphemistic description, but an accurate one as well. It was hard to move within the vast room without brushing up against someone. Right now she found herself brushing up against a sophisticated, handsome man with sea-blue eyes, light-blond hair worn like a lion's mane and a killer smile.

The latter seemed to burrow itself right into her very bones, bones that were currently experiencing, for lack of a better description, a startling jolt of electricity.

He was tall, very tall. At six-one or six-two he dwarfed her, despite her four-inch heels. He also filled out his deep-gray suit to perfection with shoulders that in an emergency she was certain could probably easily accommodate an aircraft landing.

He was definitely a man who deserved to be regarded as one of the beautiful people, she mused, studying him as she took a slow, languid sip from the champagne flute she was holding.

Cocking her head, she glanced back at the sculpture. "It looks as if it was done yesterday."

Very few things threatened to make Cole's heart stop. This, however, was one of them. Just who *was* she? Had she been sent by the person responsible for the statue's disappearance? Was she here to expose him?

Cole kept his cool as he quietly asked, "I beg your pardon?"

Waves of unease reached Elizabeth. She'd startled him for some reason. Why? Her observation was harmless.

Wasn't it?

"The timelessness," she clarified, watching him more closely now. "The sculpture looks as if it could have been created in this century instead of 1862."

"You're familiar with the work, then?"

"With the artist," she amended. "I know that Auguste Rodin was heartbroken when his sister died and this was his way of honoring her. It's the first known piece he ever did."

She got nothing more. The waves she'd thought she

detected had faded. Her imagination? Maybe her new-found freedom was playing havoc with her perception.

"A pity," she went on, "that it's been hidden all this time."

So, she was an art enthusiast. Cole felt a little relieved. Right now, he was more interested in her than in the sculpture. "Speaking of being hidden, why haven't I seen you before at one of these openings?"

Her smile was slow, he thought, like early-morning heat in New Orleans, spreading languidly, poking invasive fingers into the shadows. "Maybe you weren't looking."

Her voice was like Southern Comfort being poured into a tall glass, thick, smooth. It suited her.

The undercurrent of excitement didn't leave.

"Trust me, you're not the type to be overlooked." He extended his free hand to her. "Cole Williams."

She raised her eyes to his, innocence and sin mingled in equal proportions. It went with the smile. "Yes, I know who you are. Ariel Lockwood." She told him the name that was on the invitation. The woman had connections to the world of the rich and famous, but was currently in Europe, according to something she remembered reading. That meant she couldn't put in a sudden appearance. "And is that your best line?"

He laughed softly, keeping his other thoughts from registering on his face.

"Does sound like a line, doesn't it?" He subdued the urge to slip his arm around her waist and guide her to a more private corner. There *was* no more private corner. He didn't need a head count to know that everyone who had gotten an invitation had shown up. "But it's not a line," he assured her. "It's merely an observation. Where are you from?"

Because the din had increased, she leaned into him before answering, "Here and there."

Magnetism, that's what she had, he thought. The fact that he felt it intrigued him. "I'm acquainted with the life. Jet-setting on Daddy's money, or your own?"

She raised her chin and he saw the pride in her eyes. That, too, was something he was acquainted with. "My own. Definitely my own."

Cole paused to take a sip of his champagne. As he did so, he looked around, anticipating being the target of unveiled daggers. But there was only envy in the eyes of the men who were close enough to inhale the pricey fragrance the woman in red was wearing.

In control of every situation he'd ever been in, Cole felt the stirrings of possessiveness taking hold. It surprised him.

"Are you here with anyone?" Even as he asked, he couldn't imagine an exquisite creature like this woman being alone.

Elizabeth smiled up into his face. "Right now I'm with you."

Her smile was working its way under his skin. Heating his blood. He began to wonder what it would be like to make love with her. He could see those long nails of hers raking his flesh. Nails as red as the dress she was wearing. "I mean, did you come with anyone?"

Knowing the value of mystery, she said, "Not this time."

The disappointment that reared its head was a complete surprise. "But there is someone."

She thought of Anthony, who had always been such a part of her life. There'd never been a time when she'd been without him. He would have insisted on coming with her to the gala, even though art held no allure for him. Protecting her from the world, however, did.

"There is someone," she told him, the words leaving her lips casually. "But we've come to a parting of the ways."

He pitied the man who had lost her. "Must be my lucky day."

Her eyes touched his. He could all but feel them making contact. She was bewitching him.

"There you go," she said softly, the words rippling on his skin, "resorting to lines again."

He definitely wanted to make love with this woman. Cole lowered his face so that his lips were just by her ear.

"The funny thing about lines is that they're entrenched in the truth. Repeated too often, they become clichéd. But that doesn't make them any less true."

Straightening, Cole saw Harold Reiner waving a raised hand in his direction. The CEO of one of his holding companies was beckoning him over to a semicircle of some rather heavy-duty investors in the media empire he'd fashioned. A small frown crossed his lips. He was no one's lackey, but he'd gotten where he was by keeping his ear to the ground and paying strict attention to the noises he heard, ably differentiating between the ones that required attention and the ones that were strictly noise.

Time to discover which was which.

A sigh escaped his lips. Any further exchange between him and this lovely creature was going to have to be put on hold temporarily. "If you'll excuse me for a moment, duty calls."

Elizabeth followed her companion's line of vision. Starved for input, she absorbed two newspapers daily and recognized the collection of men from a photograph she'd seen on the business page just yesterday.

"Heady company," she observed. Reiner gestured again. She looked back up at the man beside her. "You'd better jump."

Cole's eyes held hers for a moment. Was she putting him on or just fishing? He had no clear handle on her and that bothered him. "I never jump."

"I'll keep that in mind."

Inexplicably, anticipation traveled through him like a bullet. *Not the time,* he cautioned himself.

Inclining his head, he murmured, "To be continued," as he touched her shoulder.

The connection sent another jolt through her.

Except for the day she'd been shopping and had heard a scream echo in her head, a scream that had come from Dani's little boy, Alex, and had been uttered countless miles away, to her knowledge she'd only connected with the other triplets. To date, she'd never detected any ability to read the minds of strangers.

She hadn't really read Cole's, but she'd felt something, something she couldn't quite put into words. It was a mingling of feelings, for lack of a better description. She had no idea what was on his mind, but she'd strongly sensed his reaction to her.

Anthony's kept you out of the game much too long, she told herself. *This is nothing more than a male-female connection.*

Overprotective, Anthony would jump into the fray, acting as a human shield any time any man caught her attention for more than a fleeting second or vice versa. He was part pit bull, part chaperone, bound and determined to keep every male over the age of twelve away from her.

But Anthony wasn't here tonight and she was, Elizabeth thought with no small feeling of triumph.

Watching, she saw that Cole had found his way to the circle of men who had commandeered his attention.

For now, she turned back to the statue in order to try to figure out just what it was about the sculpture that bothered her. It was like a grain of sand embedded in her shoe, chafing her with each step she took.

As he listened to Reiner talk, Cole looked over toward the woman in red. She was frowning slightly as she regarded the sculpture.

His biggest asset, he'd found, was not his business

acumen and his outgoing personality that allowed him to gain people's confidence easily. It was his ability to recognize trouble when he saw it.

And gorgeous though she was, something told him that this woman was trouble.

With a capital *T*.

Chapter 3

Elizabeth left her car parked more than a block away. A trickle of perspiration zigzagged down her spine as she made her way through the night toward the gallery.

The sound of her footsteps echoed in her head, resounding far more loudly there than they actually did on the street. She knew how to walk softly, how to move without disturbing anything.

She'd been carefully taught.

Okay, so this was crazy, Elizabeth readily admitted. And there was no real reason for it.

None except to satisfy her own curiosity. And because she'd challenged herself.

Just to see if she could do it.

Adrenaline raced through her veins, making her high with excitement, with anticipation. When the end was in doubt—and there was always a doubt—the rush was that much more intense. Her pulse throbbed. Essentially, this was her first non-Anthony job. And the first that hadn't been handed to them by Jeremy. There was no tangible reward in sight, no monetary gain at the end.

It didn't matter.

The danger was just as great, and the reward—well, independence was a heady condition and this would let her know whether she could go it alone if she so chose. If she had the nerve to go in without backup.

She knew she did.

She was going to break into the art gallery.

She'd remained at the gala almost to the very end. Setting her doubts about the sculpture aside, she'd mingled and talked with a variety of people, absorbing tidbits here and there and storing them away as future sources of information. She never knew when something could come in handy in her line of work.

Twice, she'd noticed, Cole Williams looked as if he was attempting to make his way back to her. Both times someone had buttonholed him, dragging him away to hold court over a group of people. Once she'd witnessed a little blonde, whose allowance only seemed to cover half a dress, hang herself off his arm until he'd handed her off to someone else. The blonde hadn't looked happy.

Busy man, that Williams, she mused.

As she made her way through the dark, deserted Philadelphia streets now, she wondered if Williams suspected that he might have a fake in the center of his collection. Although, she amended, it actually wasn't part of his collection. The plaque beside it said that *Venus Smiling* was on loan from the Jonathan MacFarland collection.

She was familiar with the name. The man was another captain of industry who liked his art. Mainly, MacFarland liked his art to be private, but according to one newspaper article, he'd been prevailed upon, because of a recent merger between one of Williams's companies and one of his own, to make a peace offering by loaning out his sculpture.

Word on the street was that the two men didn't exactly get along. As she recalled, it had something to do with early days, Williams's code of honor and MacFarland's apparent lack of the same.

Elizabeth stopped walking and listened. A dog, sans its master, came ambling down the block across from her. It stopped for a moment, as if debating whether she was worth crossing the street for, then obviously decided she wasn't. The animal trotted off into the night. She began walking again. Her mouth curved in a smile. She wondered what it might do to the merger if MacFarland discovered that his sculpture was a fake.

Had Cole Williams made the substitution himself? To get even for something done to him by MacFarland at an earlier date?

"Whoa, Lizzie, you're getting ahead of yourself," she cautioned under her breath as she made her way into the alley behind the gallery. "Maybe Williams is the victim. And that's *if* the thing actually is a fake.'' There was always the chance that she was wrong.

Although not likely.

She just had this *feeling* and she'd learned a long time ago not to shrug off her intuition without first exploring the cause of that reaction. Most of the time she was right.

If not for her curiosity, Elizabeth told herself as she scanned the rear exit of the gallery, this really wasn't her problem.

But, oh, this was such a challenge.

The slight trickle of perspiration was gone, dried up in the heat of her anticipation. She was primed and ready to go.

For a moment she stood before the exit, bracing herself. There was probably a guard somewhere in the building, although given the relatively small size of the place, there might not be. What there was on the premises without a doubt was a security system. Knowing Williams, it was probably a damn good one. Had this been a job commissioned by Jeremy and undertaken by Anthony and her, there would have been a maximum of preparations made. There would have been diagrams secured, schedules memorized, all contingencies weighed and measured. One to two weeks of intense work at a minimum.

There was no time for that.

She was diving into this headfirst, acting on a whim only a little while after the gala had ended and the last guest had gone home.

She'd gone home herself, never connecting again

with Williams. Maybe if she had, she wouldn't have returned here.

Who was she kidding? She would have come back. Curiosity was one of her best attributes, along with tenacity.

She'd changed her clothes, putting on all black attire, and given it a couple of hours before returning. By the time she had, the caterers and cleaning crews had all left. The place looked deserted. There were floodlights at the front entrance, where the gallery faced the world. The rear of the gallery, however, was cast in almost pitch darkness.

There was no moon tonight, allowing her to blend in with the shadows.

It was time to get started.

"All systems go," she whispered to herself.

Elizabeth stared at the lock on the rear door. It appeared to be a simple padlock. If it was, that was only because the security inside was probably so great, she reasoned. The padlock almost dared a thief to come in and try his luck.

Well, she wasn't a thief. At least, not tonight. But she had never let a dare go unanswered, not even as a child. She had the scars to prove it. But that had been before she'd learned something about herself and how to use her unique abilities.

Elizabeth reverted to them now. Staring at the lock, she began to concentrate, focusing all of her thoughts, all her energy, on the shiny metal object. Her breathing slowed. She could literally feel her blood slow down in her veins. It was as if all her systems were being channeled into this one object.

The lock shuddered, opened and fell off.

Coming to, she caught the lock in her gloved hand before it hit the ground. She set it aside and blew out a long breath. The easy part was over.

Closing her eyes for better concentration, she felt around the perimeter of the door. Satisfied that nothing would be tripped if she opened it, she eased it forward, then quickly stepped inside.

From where she stood, she could see the main room of the gallery. The statue, up on its alabaster pedestal, was still bathed in lights. Obviously not for effect. To throw off a thief?

Were the lights part of the security, or just a decoy for the real thing?

Reaching into the shoulder bag she'd brought with her, Elizabeth took out a pair of dark glasses. To the casual observer, they looked like sunglasses, but they actually allowed her to see the different ultraviolet rays that bounced around undetectable to the naked eye.

Just as she thought. The statue stood in the center of an elaborate crisscross pattern of lights. Breaking any stream would trip the alarm system.

Elaborate, but not impossible. Especially not for someone as agile as she. Elizabeth smiled to herself as she set down the shoulder bag.

Show time.

Stepping over, under, around and through, looking like a dancer executing enormously complex steps, she managed to avoid every ray, every sensor that could set off the alarm. Her body screamed as she moved in slow motion, holding poses until she was certain of her next step.

Had this been one of their routine assignments, either she or Anthony would have gotten the location of the power source for the security system. Then she would have disabled it, exercising the same energy she'd used on the padlock. Even after all these years, she still didn't know the full range of her telekinetic abilities. She knew she could move small objects by concentrating on them. Of late, she'd found she could do the same with larger objects. They just required more concentration. But was there a limit to her power, or was it merely bound by her ability to concentrate?

After what seemed an eternity, she'd managed to get next to the sculpture without breaking any of the beams. The high-intensity light she had shoved in her pocket she now shone on the object. It allowed her to thoroughly scrutinize the statue.

There was no nick. The original, Jeremy had once mentioned to her, because he'd been fortunate enough to actually see the statue before MacFarland had it taken away from public view, had just the vaguest nick at the bottom of her gown. But there was no nick and no indication that one had been doctored.

It was just as she thought. Venus might be smiling, but she was also a fake.

Suddenly, the lights went on, flooding the room. Caught by surprise and momentarily blinded, Elizabeth swung around. Her mind whirled about frantically, searching for a plausible explanation for what she was doing here, dressed like a burglar and standing next to a priceless work of art.

She saw the man who had thrown on the lights, and her mouth dropped open.

"Nice to see you again, 'Ariel.'"

Cole Williams, still wearing the suit he'd had on for the gala, crossed over to her. He'd been in the shadows, standing in the doorway of one of the lesser rooms, watching as she had gone through her elaborate dance, her sleek body highlighted by the blue rays that encircled the statue.

He'd never seen anything so damn sensual in his life. His body had hummed, just watching her.

After she'd introduced herself to him, he'd had a strong hunch that she'd be back. Since his hunches were usually right, he'd learned not to disregard them out of hand.

Elizabeth concentrated on looking cool. "There is an explanation."

"And I'd be interested in hearing it." He beckoned her forward. When she made no move to come closer, he said, "Don't worry, I've turned off the security system around the statue." A sensual smile curved his mouth. "There doesn't seem to be a point in keeping it on, although I have to admit I would like to see that little dance of yours again." His eyes washed over her body. "It was very stimulating."

She raised her chin a fraction of an inch. "What are you doing here?"

Talk about a cool customer, he mused. This lady certainly took the prize. "I could ask you the same thing."

"I asked first."

Bravado, that was the word for it. He felt a kernel of admiration stirring. Growing. "I've never met a thief as brazen as you."

She squared her shoulders, wondering if he was playing with her. Had he called the police? No, he seemed too laid-back for that. Besides, by now she'd be hearing sirens in the distance.

"And you still haven't. I'm not a thief." *At least not technically,* she added silently.

"Right." His eyes slid toward the sculpture. "Because you didn't get away with it."

"I wasn't trying to get away with it." She had a feeling that he knew that.

Amusement entered his eyes. "So then, what, you were here to dust it? I have a cleaning crew. They're very thorough."

How thorough? she wondered. "Then maybe they're the ones who took it."

"Took it?" The amusement faded, replaced by an edge in his voice.

They were shadowboxing. It was time to take a real swing. "Your statue is a fake."

He was right. She was a professional. "And how would you know that? Being a fake yourself?"

She opened her mouth to answer, and he had this sudden, overwhelming and completely ridiculous urge to sweep her into his arms and kiss her. If he did, he wondered who would be more surprised, her or him. Hormones had never been a problem for him. They'd never ruled him. He enjoyed his passions, but only when he felt like indulging them.

Now, however, he felt that his reactions were in control of him rather than the other way around. He didn't like that.

"You see," he said, cutting off any story she might begin to weave. "I met the real Ariel Lockwood years ago." Crossing his arms before him, he regarded her figure. "If she could have had your body, I'm sure she would have paid any amount of money for it. The woman stands about five foot eleven squared, and on her last birthday there were sixty-three candles on her cake. Now, unless you stumbled across the fountain of youth, I believe it's safe to say that you are not Ariel Lockwood."

"No," Elizabeth agreed with a slight inclination of her head as she conceded the point. "I'm not."

What she was, Cole thought, was incredibly cool. Here she was, literally busted and yet she looked and sounded as if they were discussing nothing more serious than what she'd had for lunch that afternoon.

She was also not forthcoming with her identity. "Then who are you?"

"Someone who knows that this is a fake."

He frowned. If she'd noticed, then maybe someone else had, too, although no one had said anything to him. MacFarland had stopped by for less than half an hour, a goodwill appearance on his part, and although he'd only spared a cursory glance at the statue, he seemed to accept it.

"What gave it away?" Cole asked.

Her smile was slow, reaching her eyes several beats after it appeared.

"Then you know." She looked over her shoulder at the statue. It was beautiful. "It's flawless, which is ultimately the problem. There should be a nick right about there," she pointed. She looked back at him and asked guilelessly, "Are you trying to pull off a scam?"

He studied her for a long moment, weighing options. On a whim, he decided to trust her. A little. "I'm trying to buy some time."

Elizabeth came to the only logical conclusion she saw opened to her. "I take it someone stole the sculpture from you?"

"Before the opening." His eyes slid over her. It was difficult making an impartial judgment about the woman before him when she was causing some very non-impartial stirrings within him. "If you know the statue is a fake, why are you trying to steal it?"

"I told you, I'm not trying to steal it. I just wanted to find out if I was right."

He still had his doubts about the veracity of her claim. "So you went to all this trouble, breaking into the gallery, risking getting caught, just to find out if you'd guessed correctly?" His expression bordered on incredulous.

Elizabeth raised her slim shoulders in a half shrug. "I don't see it as trouble."

Which could only mean one thing. "You do this for a living." It wasn't a question, it was an assumption. Cole saw a barrier come down in her eyes. It came complete with a No Trespassing sign. Who was she? He wanted answers and it looked as if he was going to have to resort to threats in order to get them. "You realize I can have you arrested for breaking and entering."

"But you won't."

She looked pretty damn confident of that. He wasn't accustomed to being ignored, or outplayed. It got under his skin.

"And why won't I?"

Leaving his side, she placed herself before a small canvas, a sketch done by Michelangelo, recently discovered and sold in auction for a million and a half. Regarding it for a moment and still not answering him, she turned her attention to another painting. She moved about as coolly as if they were conducting a discussion about the merits of one artist over another.

Finally, she said, "Because you can't risk the scandal of anyone finding out the statue is a fake. Otherwise, you wouldn't have gone through this elaborate charade of having a fake—a very good one I might add—in its place." She paused, then looked back again at the statue. "Whom did you use? Lorenzo?"

By plucking the name out of the air, she'd done it to him again. She'd managed to surprise him. Cole didn't know whether to take his hat off to her in admiration, or get her as far away from him as possible.

His curiosity tipped the scale for him. "How would you know about Lorenzo?"

They had worked together a time or two. The older master had been her mentor, teaching her how best to make her work pass as authentic. "Let's just say it's a small world."

"Not small enough." His eyes met hers. "I still don't know who you are."

Even if Anthony hadn't impressed her with the need, time and again, there were some areas where she exercised extreme caution.

"And maybe it should stay that way." She saw the suspicion in Cole's eyes. "Don't worry, I won't tell anyone about your little secret. I don't want your reputation besmirched." She smiled beguilingly. "There's nothing in it for me."

He studied her carefully. And made a judgment call. "How about if there was something in it for you?"

She cocked her head, trying to divine just what it was he was getting at. "You're not talking about sullying your reputation, are you?"

Smart lady, she picked up on that, he thought. "No, I'm talking about preserving it."

Exercising caution, she slowly waltzed around the subject, neither committing nor rejecting until she knew exactly what he was driving at. "And just how would I do that?"

He'd already decided that he was going to need help beyond what he already employed. That meant bringing in an unknown. No one fit the description better than this woman, who was still an unknown to him. "By helping me find out who stole the real statue. And then getting it back."

She waited for the other shoe to drop. "And I would do this because…"

"I'd pay you."

Cole saw a light come into her eyes and found himself struggling not to be drawn in. The situation struck him as rather humorous. He was a six-foot-two man who was discovering what it felt like to be a moth. And her incredibly beautiful green eyes were the flame.

A job. He was offering her a job. On her own. *Take that, Anthony,* she thought. *See, not everyone thinks I'm incompetent on my own.*

She did her best to keep the glee out of her voice. "How much?"

Pragmatic. He liked that. He found he liked a great deal about this woman with no name. Ordinarily, before he struck a bargain with someone, he had them checked out. Dealing with MacFarland originally had taught him to be cautious. The exception to that had been Lorenzo. And since she was acquainted with Lorenzo, he thought it rather ironic that he was entering into an arrangement with her under the same circumstances.

He needed someone and she seemed to fit the bill.

"How much do you usually get?"

She thought it wise to qualify her statement. "That's assuming I do this kind of thing."

He grinned, and she found her stomach experiencing a strange earthquake.

"I think we've already established that," Cole said. "I don't know how you got past the lock on the back door. The heat from a hand, or the contact of metal on metal, like bull cutters, sets off an internal alarm. But nothing went off inside when you came in." He made a note to check the surveillance tape first chance he got. She might not have noticed the tiny camera he had positioned on the opposite wall of the alley. "So that means you're a professional and good at your job. I don't know if your little floor show's part of it—"

"That was impromptu, as was coming here after hours," she cut in. "I told you, I wasn't out to take the statue, just to satisfy my curiosity."

That still didn't make any sense to him. It smacked of a recklessness he was going to have to make sure she kept under control while working for him. "And that's worth a jail sentence?"

"I wasn't planning on getting caught." She looked up at Cole, her eyes challenging him.

"But you were."

It was a matter of semantics. "Only in the strictest sense of the word."

Cole had a feeling that she would eagerly argue an opponent into submission. More interested in finding the real statue, he switched gears.

"Does that mean you're going to help me?"

Although the man before her intrigued Elizabeth more than anyone she'd come across in quite some time, she didn't want to appear desperate for a job. That would leave her holding no cards and it was all about control now. Having left Anthony, she wasn't about to hand over the reins to another man.

"We'll talk."

The smile she gave him made him want to do more than just talk. A great deal more.

He was right, Cole thought as he led the way out of the room. The lady was trouble. But trouble, he had to admit, had never looked quite so inviting or intriguing before.

Chapter 4

Leading the way, Cole brought her into a small but tastefully furnished office that was a little way off the main room.

The highly polished wooden floor was new, the Napoleon brandy he poured and offered her was old. Accepting it, Elizabeth sat down in the chair that was positioned before his desk.

All in all, Elizabeth felt very comfortable in a world in which she knew she really didn't belong. For the moment she did and there was nothing wrong with pretending. Pretense made a wonderful bridge from here to there. She'd gotten through a great many situations that way.

Nursing her drink, very aware of the man who was studying her, Elizabeth carefully took in her surroundings without appearing even to be aware of them. An-

other talent she'd honed while under Jeremy's tute-
lage. She was actively alert to all possibilities,
including the one represented by the man in the room.

Before ever entering the gallery, she'd gone out of
her way to learn as much as she could about Cole
Williams. It was in keeping with the fact that she
made it a point never to walk into anything without
first knowing something about either the person she
was dealing with or the place she was venturing into.
Survival often depended on it.

Williams had begun small, taking a minor inheri-
tance left to him by his late mother and parlaying it
into a large nest egg. Buying and selling choice companies and surrounding himself with the right people,
he'd turned that money into a veritable fortune. According to the latest financial magazines, Cole Williams was easily one of the ten richest men in the
country, owning a cable network as well as a publishing empire, all well before the age of forty.

From the looks of him, Elizabeth judged that he
was a regular visitor to the gym he owned.

Raising her eyes from his hard, muscular form and
looking up into his eyes, she saw a man who was
confident, who knew his own destiny because he was
in charge of making it happen. And like a man who
dictated his own terms and got what he wanted, he
needed to be in control of things.

Just like her brother.

Just like, in his own way, Jeremy. Except that,
these days, the latter had a lighter touch. Her one-
time mentor and guardian had evolved into more of

a benevolent figure. The terms of each assignment were his, but unlike Anthony, Jeremy allowed for some flexibility. He gave her credit for having a mind, for having good sense, which was why she hadn't left Jeremy's organization, she had just elected to take a brief vacation.

Matters with her brother, however, were still very much up in the air. And would continue to be, she thought, until Anthony began treating her like an equal and not like the little sister whose every move he felt he had a right to dictate.

This wasn't a time to think about her brother, Elizabeth told herself, not when those incredible light-blue eyes were looking at her, taking measure. What was Williams thinking? Not for the first time, she lamented the fact that her talents didn't run to mind reading.

Elizabeth cupped her glass between her hands, slowly warming the sides with her skin. Waiting for Williams to make the first move.

It wasn't long in coming.

"So," he pressed when she said nothing to cut into the silence. "Who are you?"

Cole had never seen innocence mixed with sensuality before. The woman sitting in front of him pulled it off flawlessly. As regal as a queen, as tempting as sin, she was definitely a woman who could keep a man guessing.

"Just an art lover."

He laughed dryly. "You're a great deal more than that. Most art lovers don't break into art galleries after hours just to verify the authenticity of a piece.'' He knew she couldn't argue with him, but as a preventative measure, he added a coda. ''They haven't the talent.''

She smiled at him and he felt the effect rippling into his inner core.

''I've always been a little...different,'' Elizabeth allowed, then paused to take a sip of brandy. Her smile became more seductive, less innocent. ''Very good,'' she murmured as she felt the thick liquid curling through her system.

Her husky voice wound into his. It took Cole a moment to find his tongue. ''It should be, considering the cost.''

''Do you?'' she asked, raising a perfectly shaped eyebrow in response. Did he know exactly what he was worth and want more? Or had money become something that was now just there to him, to be used to facilitate the pursuit of other things? ''Consider the cost?''

It had been a long time since he'd looked at a price tag. ''Only in so much as I like having the best.'' He looked at her significantly. She was still evading him. ''So, what do I call you?''

She lifted a thin shoulder. ''Whatever you like, as long as it's not insulting.''

He laughed out loud at that. He was enjoying himself. ''I meant your name. What name do I use when I talk to you?''

For some reason, terms of endearment flocked into her head like so many sparrows looking for a place to land. She deliberately blocked them. This wasn't a man to give affection to. This was a man to be wary of. Even if he did possess a face and body that could generate endless dreams.

"Whatever you like."

He leaned his face in close to hers. For a moment, their breaths mingled. "What I'd like is to use your real name."

That rush was beginning again, the same rush she felt at the start of a job. The same kind she'd felt standing in the alley just before she'd made the lock open. It took effort to keep it from taking over.

"So that you can check me out?" she guessed, congratulating herself on how cool she'd kept her voice, especially when everything inside her felt as if it was red hot and jumping around. She noted the way Williams was looking at the brandy in her hand. "I know you're very thorough, but it really won't do you any good to have the glass checked for fingerprints." Her smile widened ever so slightly as she looked up into his eyes. She could see that the thought had crossed his mind. "I have no priors, no arrests." Her eyes teased his. "I am as pure as the driven snow."

He thought of the impression she'd made when she'd first walked into the gallery. Every man in the vicinity had stopped and looked. Every move she made whispered the promise of sex and sensuality. That was a long way from purity.

"Humor me," he urged quietly.

Right now, she would have been willing to do a

great deal more than that. Very subtly, she let go of the breath she was holding. "My name is Elizabeth."

They were too close. For his good, not hers. Straightening, Cole placed a little distance between them. "Elizabeth what?"

She paused for a moment, as if deciding whether or not to tell him, then finally said, "Caldwell."

Was she lying? He couldn't tell. She didn't flinch under scrutiny. Something else to admire about her, he thought.

Elizabeth Caldwell. He didn't know if it fit her or not. "Is that the name Lorenzo will tell me if I ask?"

Her look was complacent, confident. "If you ask, Lorenzo won't tell you anything."

"Why?" Intrigued far more than he was comfortable about, Cole pressed her for an answer. "Because there's honor among thieves and they stick together?"

She thought of the artist, his browned fingers nimbly creating, his thick gray hair, worn long and caught back against his neck. He looked like a hidalgo of old and had the honor to match. But it wasn't honor she was referring to at the moment.

"Lorenzo isn't a thief and neither am I. He won't tell you anything because he doesn't know my last name. He didn't want to know it." The less information a confidant possessed, the less risk he ran of getting into trouble for someone else's sins. "He calls me Gypsy."

Gypsy. That fit her perfectly, Cole thought. With very little effort, he could see her dancing around a campfire barefoot, a rainbow of bracelets surrounding her wrists. She'd have a tambourine in her hand and a colorful, swirling skirt around her hips with a gauzy peasant blouse clinging to her breasts. Her skin would be gleaming from the firelight.

His fingers tightened around his glass. He loosened them before he snapped the stem.

"It suits you."

"If you're trying to play to my vanity…" Elizabeth let her voice drift off for a moment as she pulled the clip out of her hair. It came cascading down about her shoulders like black velvet. "You should know that I haven't any."

His breath had caught in his throat. It took effort to draw his eyes away from her hair. She certainly did know how to get a reaction out of a man, he thought. "A woman as beautiful as you?"

"No vanity," she repeated, never taking her eyes off his face. "Just knowledge."

He felt himself being reeled in, curiosity mingled with desire, each strong in its own right. "Knowledge?"

"Of my strengths, of my weaknesses." Her eyes held his over the rim of the glass. "Knowledge of how to read the other person."

The more he listened to her, the more certain he became that he could definitely use her in this less-than-aboveboard situation he found himself in.

But he needed to keep his mind on business, not on the way her body would feel beneath his. From where he stood, that wasn't going to be easy.

It was time to solidify things before he found himself slipping off the ledge he was standing on. "About my offer, Elizabeth—"

She twirled the stem of her glass slowly. The liquid inside moved, leaving its imprint along the glass. "As I recall, you never actually made me an offer. Just hinted at it."

Cole sat down at the edge of his desk, folding his hands together as he looked down at her. "I'll pay you half a million dollars to help me get the real statue back."

Instead of answering, Elizabeth rose from her chair. As he watched, she perched on the desk beside him. She wasn't about to let him get the upper hand, and allowing him to look down at her during negotiations would silently give it to him. "You must want that statue back awfully badly."

He wasn't accustomed to explaining himself, but just this once, he made an exception. "I want my reputation intact and I'm willing to pay for it. Besides, time is of the essence. We have a little more than a week before the statue is to go back to its rightful owner." He had his men out on it, but he had a feeling that if there was a solution to his problem, he was looking at it. "So, 'Elizabeth,' will you help me?"

Something in his tone caught her attention. "You say my name as if you don't believe it's real."

There was a fifty-fifty chance she was lying to him. "I've only got your word for it."

Elizabeth pretended to take his words under consideration. "So, by your own admission, you're about to enter into a bargain with a woman whose identity you're unsure of.''

"Yes." *But I mean to find out who you are, Gypsy. I mean to.*

There was something about the way he said the word that put her on her guard. "Seems to me that's an awful lot of money to offer to a person you know nothing about.''

"I don't know who you are," he repeated, wanting to clarify the issue. "But that doesn't mean I don't know anything about you.''

Her eyes never gave away that he'd managed to confuse her. She smiled at him. "That's going to require a little more explanation.''

"I pride myself on being a very good judge of people. You worked that room the second you came in, drawing information out of people, making them *want* to tell you things.''

So, Williams hadn't rejoined her at the gala for a reason, she realized. He'd been observing her.

"You didn't fade into the background like some," he continued, "absorbing things that the rest of the people around you don't even realize they're doing or saying. You made people volunteer things.'' That in itself was a talent. But there was more. "*And* you got in here without tripping the alarm.''

"Obviously I must have tripped off some kind of alarm, or you wouldn't have been here waiting for me. Come to think of it, why *were* you waiting for me?''

"Well, for one thing, you weren't Ariel Lockwood.'' That had set off his internal alarm. But rather than let the impostor know he was on to her, or get in touch with the police, he'd opted to see what she was up to. But even that hadn't been the main reason he was here. His staying on after everyone else had left had a great deal to do with the look in her eyes as she'd studied the sculpture. There was something there that told him this was a woman to be wary of.

Because her hair had fallen into her face, Elizabeth tossed her head, sending it pooling over her shoulder. She was aware of the effect that had on the man watching her. Then, still seated on the desk, she turned her body in toward his. Balance had to be restored—and perhaps tipped in her favor. Especially if she was going to work with Williams.

''All right,'' she said smoothly. ''If you're such a good judge of people, what am I going to do next?''

She was sitting so close to him, Cole could feel the heat of her body radiating out to him. Calling to him. Or was that just his own, responding to hers? He wasn't sure. Didn't care.

He knew what he wanted to do next, but it went against the first cardinal rule he'd imposed on himself when he'd begun his quest for the better life: Never mix business with pleasure.

Up until now, that had never been a problem. He had far too much self-restraint, was far too focused, too driven, to allow things like dalliances to get in the way of his goals. To cloud his thinking so that he couldn't focus on those goals.

But this time it was different.

"I'm not sure," he told her quietly.

His voice rumbled along her skin like tiny shock waves being set off. This time she made sure her smile went straight to his gut. She was taking no prisoners. "Honesty. I like that in a man."

He found himself holding his breath. "What else do you like in a man?"

Elizabeth looked at him for a long, long moment, and tilted her face up to his in silent invitation. "Surprises."

It was as if she was pulling him in. He'd always thought of himself as an immovable object, as someone who couldn't be swayed toward a path if he didn't want to be. And maybe that was it, maybe he did want to be swayed, did want to be persuaded. To be moved from his position.

Right now he couldn't say one way or the other. All he knew was that he didn't have the ironclad control over his mind and body he'd had for as far back as he could remember.

It disturbed the hell out of him.

It didn't stop him.

Shifting so that he faced her, Cole slipped his fingers into her hair, framing her face with his hands. He felt the pull intensify, but didn't fight it. He wasn't sure he could have if he wanted to.

And he didn't want to.

His mouth came down on hers because he had no choice. He *needed* to find out what her lips tasted like, what *she* tasted like. Whether she was as utterly heady as he thought or if, for some reason, he was suffering from battle fatigue.

He hadn't taken a day off in eighteen months. His friends had all warned him, said that all work and no play would catch up to him and take its toll. And maybe it finally had.

And this was the price he had to pay.

Hell, as far as prices went, he would pay this one gladly.

His head spun. She tasted of sin. Sin and temptation and Napoleon brandy. And he felt as if he couldn't get enough of any of it.

The kiss deepened even as he felt himself growing more and more intoxicated. He'd always known when to walk away before. The only difference was, this time he wasn't walking.

Cole believed in being clearheaded at all times. But what he believed was definitely at odds with what he wanted.

What he wanted was her.

She'd wanted him to kiss her, wanted to bring him to her. To Elizabeth this represented a struggle for control, for being the one to call the shots, pure and simple. And as long as she orchestrated that, kissed him on her terms, she'd have the upper hand.

So why did she feel as if she was going under for the third time?

There was a lesson to be learned here. The proverb echoed vaguely in her brain, something about pride going before a fall. She'd been a little too confident in her abilities to hold her own, to remain unaffected even as she wound a web around a man. Around *this* man. Right now her thoughts were colliding with one another like drunken sailors on a three-day pass after nine months at sea.

Elizabeth could feel every single fiber of her body, of her very being, responding to the deep, masculine taste of him.

She wanted more.

Darkness encompassed her. Darkness with swirling lights at the heart of it, whirling around faster and faster as the pressure of his mouth bore down on her, taking her to places she'd never been.

Her pulse, already racing, began to rival an engine traveling at top speed on the autobahn. So much for being able to keep the upper hand.

Her mouth sealed to his, her senses swimming, Elizabeth was vaguely aware of Cole bringing her up to her feet. She found her body cleaving to his. Found his arms around her, pressing her into him.

Heat was flaring through her so urgently, so hard, she was surprised her clothes hadn't burned away in the process.

A moan escaped her lips.

Elizabeth wound her arms around his neck, although she had to stand on her toes to do so. The movement of her body rubbing against his was like a match striking the side of a tinderbox and then being thrown into dry brush.

The flame was instant.

For one moment, Cole thought like the adolescent he'd never been. Thought briefly of sweeping away the few things on the desk so that he could lie with her there. Be with her there.

Take her there.

Or have her take him.

The realization that he had no upper hand here, that she'd played this out to her own melody and had him dancing to her tune, had Cole urgently taking stock of himself, of the situation.

He was on board a runaway freight train and he desperately needed to pull the emergency brake while his hands still worked.

While his mind still functioned in some small, shallow way.

If he didn't, she was going to eventually toss him from that train and run right over him. As she'd so boldly pointed out, he didn't know that much about her. Maybe she was working for someone. Maybe this was all some kind of elaborate plan to bring him to his knees.

As if he wasn't already there.

He knew that right now he couldn't afford to trust anything that was going on inside of him. Most of all, he couldn't allow himself to trust the woman who had brought this all about.

Not until he had more information. Verified information. She had to be a blip in someone's life somewhere. Because she was causing a hell of a blip in his.

Taking a deep breath, he drew his head back, terminating the ride. He could feel the pulse throbbing in his throat, could feel other pulses throbbing throughout the rest of his body. Urging him to return.

Urging him to make love with her.

Which was exactly why he couldn't. Not until the job was over.

What the hell *was* this? She felt like someone just getting over a devastating attack of the flu. None of her limbs felt as if they belonged to her. With a mighty effort, Elizabeth struggled to get hold of herself. It was as if her very body was facing complete meltdown.

Air rushed into her depleted lungs. She held it there for a long moment before releasing it, hoping that it didn't sound as if she was panting.

Elizabeth tossed her head, trying for nonchalance, secretly surprised that it didn't just snap off her neck and roll away. She felt that fragile. But one look at him told her Williams didn't realize what was going on inside her. Which meant she was a better actress than she thought.

"Well, glad we got that out of the way," she said in the most cavalier voice she could manage.

He cleared his throat. She was a damn sight more affected than she was letting on. No one could kiss like that and remain distant. Well, two could play her game. "Yes, me, too."

And then he looked at her. If Elizabeth Caldwell, or whatever her name was, could affect him this way, it was practically guaranteed that she would affect any other man in the same manner. It was like having a secret weapon in his hip pocket.

He was smiling at her, she thought, as if he knew something she didn't. As if he suspected just how deeply he'd shaken up her world. She was going to have to watch that, she cautioned herself. Otherwise, Anthony would be proven right; she did need a protector standing over her, protecting her from the world.

Protecting her from herself.

I can protect myself, Anthony. Even from myself. At least, she fervently hoped so.

Chapter 5

The woman had very nearly set off her own earth-quake, Cole thought but she really still hadn't answered him.

"Am I correct in assuming that we have a deal?" He put his hand out, waiting for hers.

Elizabeth looked down at his hand. It was the kind that belonged to a man who toiled with his brain rather than his brawn. Because she'd been carefully schooled, she hesitated a moment. Heaven knew she'd more than touched her lips to his, but a hand-shake, well, that was something else again. That still meant something in the circles she frequented. It represented her word, her bond.

That couldn't be done recklessly.

As the kiss had been.

Finally, she slipped her hand into his. After all, it

was a great deal of money they were talking about. And it would be a good test of her abilities—solo. "We have a deal."

Cole nodded, noting that her handshake was firm, sure. Strong. And because it was, he felt that he needed to set the ground rules at the very start.

"All right, we need to have one thing straight. I give the orders. That means I control things."

Elizabeth pulled her hand back. She was right about Williams. He was just like Anthony. Another man out to dominate her every move.

Ain't gonna happen, mister, she promised him silently.

"No, we need to have one thing straight," she said, echoing his phrase. "You tell me the parameters and hand me the canvas. I paint on it." Her eyes narrowed just a little. "And I don't do well on a leash."

The woman was raising images in his head again, hot, steamy images that had no place here and now. Later, when this was behind them, he knew he wanted to avail himself of her, to see if she lived up to the promise he'd just sampled, but now wasn't the time.

Cole inclined his head. "I'll remember to keep that in mind."

"Do that." She looked at him, wondering if she'd just made a deal with the devil. They said that Lucifer was the most beautiful of the archangels. And the one to be most leery of.

But this was her maiden run and, for better or for worse, she'd struck a bargain. She meant to be the one who came out on top.

Because she was also pragmatic, Elizabeth got down to business. "Now, then, do you have any idea who might have taken the statue?"

Cole laughed softly as he poured himself another drink. He raised his brow in her direction, but she shook her head, declining another brandy. She wanted a clear head from here on. Kissing him had rattled her enough, she didn't need anything more to taint her perception. "You mean do I have any enemies? Anyone in my position has enemies."

Elizabeth nodded. She knew all about that. A back issue of *Time* magazine in the library had told her as much. "And you have more than most. The vindictive kind, if I'm not mistaken."

When she paused, he beckoned, as if coaxing more words out of her. His grin was amused. Inviting. She was determined not to get lost in it. "Come on, impress me some more."

"It wasn't done to impress you," she told him crisply. "It was homework. I always do my homework." It went hand in hand with never being unprepared. Accidents had a nasty habit of happening no matter what. Being prepared cut down on the risks.

His amusement seemed to grow. "You must have gotten very good grades in school."

School, after the age of thirteen, had revolved around Jeremy and tutors he brought in. Men and women, she suspected, who came from the same walk of life, had the same frame of reference, as Jeremy did.

But she and Williams were still waltzing around

each other, still testing for weaknesses, for breaks in the walls. She gave nothing away freely. ''When it counted.''

Cole took another sip of brandy, thinking that the spirit had tasted better on her lips. ''What made you say 'vindictive'?''

He knew that better than she did, she thought. Williams was testing her. All right, she'd take his exam. ''You've shown up a lot of people, exposed them for the dirty dealings they were involved in. That doesn't get forgotten very easily—or forgiven. My guess is that there's nothing some of those people wouldn't like better than to see you covered with the same kind of mud that they wear.''

If she'd gone this far this quickly, maybe she had a hunch who was responsible, Cole thought. It didn't hurt to play along until he learned something. ''Go on.''

She didn't want to go too far out on the limb. Not too quickly, anyway. She still wasn't that sure of Williams. The articles she'd read made him out to be a straight shooter, someone whose word was his bond. But then, he had a fleet of public relations people who knew how to make him appear to be covered in roses. She wanted to form her own opinion. That meant proceeding slowly along that limb.

''That's it for now,'' she allowed. When he looked disappointed, she added, ''Except that if I were to look for the man or group responsible for the sculpture's theft, I'd begin with the man who agreed to loan you the piece in the first place.''

His eyes captured hers. Was that a random guess? Or did she know something? He still really didn't know anything about her except that she stirred him. Him and every red-blooded male within a five-mile radius. He was going to have to get in contact with Hagen and have him run as intense a check on her as was possible.

"What makes you think MacFarland is responsible?" he asked.

She shrugged. "Proximity. Access."

"All very true, except for one thing."

He was leaning over her again. She began to do multiplication tables in her head, trying to hold her reactions to him at bay. It was an old way she had of distracting herself. It usually worked. Usually. "And this is?"

"He doesn't have an ax to grind." As if declaring a time out, Cole moved back toward the bar. "The merger between our two companies was advantageous to both of us."

His answer didn't change her opinion. "Maybe he didn't want it advantageous to you both. Maybe he wanted it advantageous only to him."

He thought of Jonathan MacFarland. She might be right, although to do what she suggested would throw the whole deal into jeopardy. "I think you're going off in the wrong direction."

Maybe he did, but she didn't. The more she talked about it, the more convinced she was that she was right. As she was wont to do, Elizabeth dug in.

"Now, you see, this is where that free-will thing is going to come in. My direction, my choice."

"But it's my money. And my clock that's ticking."

She spread her hands wide. "I don't locate it, you don't pay me."

He studied Elizabeth for a moment, not sure what to make of her. "You're that confident in yourself?"

The smile on her lips told him nothing. Except that he felt like kissing her again. But that wasn't going to get him back the sculpture—or keep his good name intact. Nothing ruined a good name faster than an arrest. Even if it didn't stand up in court, people remembered the scandal, the media hype, not the outcome. He of all people was aware of that.

"I would have to be, don't you think?" she told him.

He was paying her to work for him, but he'd chosen her because of her uniqueness, which had struck him as he'd watched her get by the security beams. "All right, you look into it your way, but I want to be kept apprised of every detail."

She grinned, picking up the brandy glass again. Now she could afford to let her mind be the slightest bit cloudy. She held it up to him, waiting for him to fill it. "Wouldn't have it any other way."

Cole picked up the decanter and poured two fingers worth into her glass. He had the distinct impression she was humoring him, but that was all right, as long as the result was the same. And he meant to make sure of that. "One more thing."

She watched him retire the decanter to the bar. "And that is?"

Cole turned around to face her. She couldn't read his expression. "For the duration of this arrangement, I'd like you to remain at my mansion."

Erotic images, emerging out of nowhere, rose in her mind's eye. Remaining in close contact was one thing, staying under one roof was another. Did he want to keep close tabs on her—or was he asking for the arrangement for another reason? "Why?" she asked matter-of-factly.

Cole was playing with fire and he knew it. But there was a great deal at stake, and in the event that she turned out to be working for someone else, getting close to him so that whoever it was she owed allegiance to remained one step ahead, he wanted this woman where he could get his hands on her.

"Let's just say I believe in keeping my friends close, my enemies closer."

"Taking advice from Winston Churchill, very commendable." She smiled at him, feeling her stomach quiver just a little. "Friends and enemies," she repeated. "Which am I?"

He had no answer for that. Only a hunch. But hunches sometimes turned out to be wrong. And he was big enough to admit that, if only to himself. "I'll let you know when I figure it out."

"We'll discuss my moving in tomorrow." She needed that much time to make plans. This was a big step she was taking. Elizabeth raised her glass in a toast, clinking it with his. The adrenaline had begun rushing through her veins again. "This is going to be very interesting."

His eyes never left hers as he brought his glass to his lips. "My thoughts exactly."

Cole frowned as he listened to the voice on the other end of the telephone the next morning. He wasn't being told something he wanted to hear.

What he was being told, in essence, was nothing.

For all intents and purposes, the woman known as Elizabeth Caldwell did not exist. He was doing business with a ghost, an apparition. Granted, it was still early and Taylor Hagen, the chief investigator he'd relied on for over seven years, had merely done a preliminary search, but even those, given the man's resources, usually turned up something.

Cole glanced down at the pad on his desk. Throughout the conversation he'd been writing question marks. Annoyed, he pushed the pad aside. "All right, keep digging, there's got to be a trail somewhere."

"You know me, I don't give up until it's over," the deep baritone voice on the other end of the line assured him.

Hagen had come to him with an excellent reputation and had never disappointed him so far. If there was anything to be found, the man would find it. "Get back to me when you have something."

There was a pause, then Hagen asked, "What about the other thing?"

Cole's office was swept daily in an effort to root

out any bugs that might have been planted. Industrial espionage was alive and well, and as such had always to be kept one step ahead of. He knew this was Hagen's way of referring to the search for the missing statue. Hagen had been placed in charge of tracking it down, along with two other men. So far, he'd had no luck with that, either, which was what had prompted Cole impulsively to throw in his lot with Elizabeth.

Cole knew that Hagen felt personally responsible for the theft. It had happened on his watch.

"This is for the other thing," Cole replied.

This time, the pause was pregnant. "What do you mean?"

Because he'd always played his hands close to the vest, Cole said, "I'll let you know once you find out who she really is."

He heard a small intake of breath, but no further questions were asked. Hagen knew the rules. Cole wasn't paying his people to ask questions of him, just of everyone else.

"Got it." The connection terminated.

Cole replaced the receiver in the cradle. "So who the hell are you, Gypsy?" he murmured to himself.

The next moment his secretary was tapping on his door. The woman's knock sounded more like a small animal scratching at the door to gain access.

"Come in."

Measuring barely five feet in her shoes, Evangeline Witherspoon, fiftyish and pencil-thin, seemed dwarfed by the newspapers she was carrying into his office. With a look of relief, she placed them on his desk. There was a copy of each of the local newspapers, as well as the *New York Times* and the *Los Angeles Times*.

Her eyes were smiling as she looked at him. "They're all very favorable, Mr. Williams. The gala last night was a huge success."

He nodded, still somewhat distracted. "People rarely slam charitable events, Vangie." His new gallery's opening gala had neatly coincided with a fundraiser that he annually chaired. The fund-raiser collected money for breast cancer research, a disease he personally hoped to see eradicated in his lifetime because it had stolen away both his mother and his older sister, Lisa, decades too early.

He felt that the specter of the stolen piece of art would make everything he dealt with suspect, including the charity. Someone was out to tear him down with no regard as to the kind of repercussions something like that might have.

He wasn't going to allow it to happen.

Elizabeth was all moved in for the duration. Even though the arrangement was for only two weeks, she wasn't totally comfortable about it. Still, she could see why it would make sense. This way, Williams could remain on top of things.

As long as one of those things wasn't her.

Not that she'd mind exactly, but she wanted it on her terms, not his. And making sure the man didn't get the upper hand might take some doing on her part.

In the meantime, she had her hands more than full with this assignment. Pausing, she stretched as she sat at the computer where she'd been for the last few hours, working a magic all her own.

From what she'd discovered, Williams seemed to have dealings with the world at large. The list he'd given her this morning of people he personally thought might want to get some kind of revenge against him was incomplete. His acquisitions, though all aboveboard—at least from what she could discern at the moment—still were far from bloodless.

In each and every case, there'd been other moguls out there bidding against him. And other would-be moguls who'd had companies bought right out from under them before they could make their move. It was difficult not to have hard feelings over that, even if the man doing the acquiring had a reputation that was just a shade less rowdy than Sir Galahad.

Or maybe that was just the point, she thought suddenly.

Everyone loved discovering that the saint had feet of clay, and although Cole Williams certainly didn't kiss like anyone's idea of a saint, he was the white knight of choice for a great many causes. Even the gala last night had had a dual purpose. He had wealthy people who fancied themselves patrons of the arts opening up their pockets for a charity that touched them all in one way or another.

It had taken very little poking around on her part to discover that as his fortune had grown, so had his largesse. And although he didn't give it away as fast as he made it, he'd certainly donated more than his share. More than his *state's* share, she thought as she went over the last few years of tax forms she'd managed to access on her computer.

"You're not supposed to be checking me out."

Cole's resonant voice seemed to fill the den. She'd caught a whiff of his scent the moment he'd entered the room less than a heartbeat before he spoke. Consequently, he hadn't surprised her.

But her pulse still chose to accelerate a little.

Turning her head, Elizabeth glanced at him over her shoulder. It was close to six o'clock. She thought big executive types didn't come straggling in until the late hours of the evening. But then, Cole Williams wasn't your average executive, or even your average billionaire if half of what she'd read was true.

"I'm not. I'm checking out everyone you ever had any dealings with." She leaned back in her chair, turning it around to face him. "I've come to the conclusion that you know the immediate world."

"Not quite. I don't know you." Which was what had brought him home early. He'd half expected her not to be there. But Cummings, his housekeeper, had assured him that "the young lady is still in."

Here it comes, Elizabeth thought. "Just exactly how do you mean that?"

"You don't exist." Cole sat down on the sofa. Until he did, he hadn't realized how tired he felt. Or how tense. It felt as if he'd been doing a balancing act on a tightrope and his feet kept threatening to slip. "At least, Hagen can't find any proof that you do."

"And Hagen would be?"

"My chief investigator."

She was aware that he kept an investigative agency on retainer. "You might do better having Hagen looking into the identity of the person trying to steal your reputation."

He didn't like being dictated to, even by someone as attractive as she. When he was a kid, his teachers had all told his mother that he would never amount to anything because he never adhered to rules. But they were wrong on all counts. He didn't mind adhering to rules, as long as the rules were his own.

"Why is there no record of an Elizabeth Caldwell going to school?"

She'd been Elizabeth Payne back then. Payne had been her father's name. Caldwell was a name a well-meaning social worker had christened the three of them with in an effort to hide them in plain sight. The woman's intent had been to keep them safe from a father who was obviously deranged. It seemed to her now a wasted effort. As far as she knew, her father, a man by the name of Benedict Payne, had never attempted to find any of them in the twenty-eight years that had passed since her mother's murder.

She was mildly curious. "It's a common enough name. I would have imagined that you would have found someone who answered to it."

The woman didn't flinch, didn't blink. He would have said that there was ice water in her veins—if not for the fact that he had kissed her and had felt her heart.

"Several, as a matter of fact. But none that would have been you."

Elizabeth smiled at him before turning her attention back to the computer screen. "It's my name. It's what I answer to. And it's the name I'd like to see on the check."

"What check?"

"The check you'll make out to me once you and *Venus* exchange smiles again."

He was instantly alert, looking at the screen and searching for the source of her confidence. "Have you found something?"

"I have a feeling," she said quietly as she angled the flat panel so that he could get a better view.

He saw that she had untangled an elaborate skein of holding companies and conglomerates. Multi-colored lines crisscrossed up and down the screen like veins within a skeletal structure. She had highlighted a name for his benefit.

Leaning over her, one hand on the desk, one hand on the back of her chair, Cole read the name. "Jonathan MacFarland."

"It keeps coming back to him."

Or was it a matter of her manipulating things so that her point was proven? "I already told you, there is no bad blood between us."

"Says you."

"And you think he says differently?"

She was certain of it. Everything she'd come across in the last half hour told her she was right. "Are you aware that over the last fifteen years, MacFarland had some connection to twelve of the holding companies you've taken over?''

Names were presented to him at the time of merger, but over the years there had been so many, he hadn't taken note for longer than it took for the ink to dry on the appropriate lines.

''Still, I—''

She left no room for his protest. ''Being second-best doesn't sit well with some people. People don't like to lose, especially not to someone they feel is above them.''

Cole was confident, but to his knowledge, no one could accuse him of being vain. He certainly didn't rub people's noses in what he did. Enemies formed easily enough of their own volition; he didn't have to go out of his way to cultivate them.

''Why would he feel that?'' he asked her.

''Goodness is always above evil.''

He stared at her. ''Evil?''

She tapped the screen beneath MacFarland's name. She'd read about robber barons who were cleaner than Jonathan MacFarland.

''Jonathan MacFarland is not exactly squeaky clean. But then, he's not the exception. You are.'' Elizabeth turned the flat panel back in her direction. ''I've never come across anyone so damn pure. Where do you hang your halo at night?''

The thoughts he was having about her right now didn't even remotely place him in that angel category. What was it about this woman that aroused him so? Was it that she was a complete mystery?

"Right next to my wings," he quipped. "So you're really convinced that he has the statue?"

"As I said, I have a feeling."

There was something in the way she said it that told him she relied more heavily on these "feelings" than the average person. He had hunches of his own, and his told him he was not dealing with a woman who fit easily into any niche he was acquainted with. "Do you fancy yourself a clairvoyant?"

"Not exactly."

"Then what 'exactly'?" he pressed.

She wondered what he'd say if he knew that she was telekinetic? That objects, especially metal ones, moved for her the way they didn't for the average person? But to give him a demonstration would mean risking having him look at her as if she were some kind of freak. She'd been that route before.

"You're paying for results, Williams. Not to learn my secrets."

He could feel it again, that stirring that she created within him. "And what would I have to pay to learn your secrets?"

"I'm afraid they aren't for sale, and neither am I. Just my services," she underscored. "So if you're one of those people who thinks that everything has its price, then you're going to be sorely disappointed."

Cole studied her for a long moment. "Whatever you say."

He had a feeling that Elizabeth Caldwell, or whatever her real name was, might be many things, but disappointing was not one of them.

Chapter 6

Elizabeth swung her legs back under the desk. "If we subscribe to my theory that MacFarland is behind this," she resumed, focusing her attention back on the computer screen and away from quite possibly the most disarming eyes she had ever seen, "the switch with the crates was most likely carried out between the time the statue was loaded on the truck and the time that it was delivered to your gallery."

He shook his head. "There's only one thing wrong with that."

He would have disappointed her if he hadn't raised at least one objection. It was what made this job that much more exhilarating for her, showing him that he was wrong. "And that is?"

"Hagen saw the statue being crated up." He'd sent

the man personally to MacFarland's mansion to over-
see the packing.''

Elizabeth turned her chair to face him. Elbows
leaning against the armrests, she rocked slowly back
and forth as she studied his face. ''And you trust Hagen.''

Was that a mocking note in her voice? Or was he
just reading things into what she was saying? ''As
much as I trust anyone. I've known him for seven
years, and he's never disappointed me.''

There was always a first time. Working for Jeremy,
she'd encountered enough con artists to know that
they came in all sizes and shapes. Cole Williams
wouldn't have been the first man to be duped by an
''honest'' man. ''How's he fixed financially?''

His expression darkened. He knew where she was
heading with this. The subject of disloyalty was a sore
one. ''I pay my people well.''

She had no doubts that he did. But a great deal of
money could temporarily buy almost anyone's loyalty. ''Any outstanding debts?''

He'd heard that Hagen's wife had had a gambling
problem, but that was a while back and the man knew
he could always come to him if there was a need.
Cole did what he did best. He shored up and protected
his own. ''You're barking up the wrong tree.''

Elizabeth spread her hands wide, oozing innocence.
''Not barking, just asking questions.'' She couldn't
help adding, ''Plenty of ways to play switch-the-crate
between here and there.''

Not with Hagen accompanying the crate, Cole said

to himself. "My man followed it in his car all the way to the gallery." He leaned over her chair, one hand on either armrest, until his face was almost level with hers. "This wasn't exactly a shell game, Gypsy. The statue's a little larger than a pea."

He certainly could send her pulse racing, she thought. But this was part of the excitement of the job. With the challenge of being on her own, without Anthony or Jeremy's network to rely on.

"Twenty-four inches to be exact. Same principle, however. Statue gets crated up, loaded onto a truck, driven from one city to the next, unloaded at its destination and kept in the back room for— How long before it was unpacked?"

He shrugged, not certain of the time element. "A couple of hours."

She smiled, a masterful lawyer resting her case before a jury that was eating out of her hand. "The switch could have been done anytime."

Her smug expression got under his skin. For two cents, he would have gladly wiped it off her face. It was hard to keep his voice even, as he informed her, needlessly he thought, "There were guards."

She would have been surprised if there hadn't been. She'd already sensed that Williams was nothing if not thorough.

"So far, you're not telling me anything that's changing my mind." A little incident in Maryland rose up from her memory banks. Her smile widened. "There are always guards and there are always ways to get around them."

"How many guards did you get around?"

Her eyes were laughing at him. "Ah, now you're wandering into client confidentiality."

With a sigh, Cole straightened, then looked down at this woman he'd thrown his lot in with. He had no answers when it came to her. Just how wise was it, bringing her into his home, trusting her, even guardedly? "Just what is it that you do for a living?"

The expression on her upturned face was nothing short of beguiling. "Currently, I'm tracking down Rodin's *Venus Smiling* for a client, and when I find it, I'm stealing it back."

She was toying with him. Cole found his patience was growing just the slightest bit frayed. "And not so currently?"

"Other things," she tossed off vaguely, then because he was waiting for more, added, "I right wrongs, is that sufficient?"

She was carrying mystery a little too far. And yet, he had to admit it was reeling him in. Making him wonder about her. In this case, curiosity was a powerful aphrodisiac. "Is this where your cape pops up?"

She laughed and the sound went straight to his gut. "No, that comes later."

A part of him already felt as if he'd put in a lifetime with her. "How much later?"

She leaned back, abandoning the computer. "You know, maybe I should be charging you by the question instead of by results."

She was taking this a little too lightly. Maybe viewing it as a game worked for her, but this was not a game to him. He needed information; he had standards. "I don't like buying a pig in a poke."

Her spine stiffened just a hair. There it was again, that need to be her superior. His check at the end of this assignment didn't entitle him to think that he owned her in any way. She was her own person.

Elizabeth rose to her feet, making her point as she jabbed a finger into his chest to underscore her words. She made sure to keep a smile on her lips.

"You're not buying a pig in or out of a sack, Williams. You're buying what the pig can do for you. Let's just say I return things to their rightful owners. Does that work for you?"

His eyes swept over this commando in stiletto heels. Not for the first time, he wondered what he'd gotten himself into. But there were no regrets in the wake of the question. "I guess it'll have to, won't it?"

Score one for the home team, Elizabeth thought. She flashed a brilliant smile at him. "At the very least, it'll save a lot of time, and as you pointed out, we don't have a lot of that to spare on this." She got back to business. "What do you have Hagen doing currently?" He still seemed the likeliest candidate with access inside and, in her experience, the most likely answer was usually the right one.

Cole didn't give her an answer immediately. When he did, it was deliberately vague. "Something else."

She was impressed. There was so much he could have inserted here, yet he didn't. "You don't lie, do you? Very admirable." It wasn't hard to zero in on the truth. "You're having Hagen check me out, aren't you?"

There seemed to be no point in denying it. And Cole certainly wasn't about to apologize for it. "I like to be thorough."

"Do you also like wasting your money?"

She wandered over to the window. She couldn't begin to see the end of his property. *Must be nice,* she thought. The only land she'd ever owned was the dirt embedded in the soles of her sneakers.

For a second she looked at his reflection in the glass, then swung around to face him. "You want to know about me? Okay, here goes. I had eccentric parents who kept me out of the public-school system, which is why you couldn't find any record. They sent me off to a convent in Switzerland where some very strict little nuns saw to it that I knew my Latin."

He had his doubts about that, but he kept his expression unreadable. "Are they the ones who taught you how to break into art galleries?"

"No," she responded primly. "When I was thirteen, my parents died in a skiing accident. My uncle Jeremy took me in. He saw to it that my education was, shall we say, broadened." That was an understatement if ever there was one, she thought. Jeremy gave equal importance to learning math and learning how to dismantle an elaborate security system.

Cole gave his own interpretation of her words. "And he taught you breaking and entering." It wasn't a question.

In reply, she gave him a truism she'd learned from

Jeremy a long time ago. "He taught me that information is best appreciated and absorbed if doled out slowly." Hands on supple hips, she cocked her head. "Now then, any other questions?"

Cole laughed and shook his head. He knew no more now than when he'd begun. He doubted very much if she'd ever seen the inside of a convent, in Switzerland or out of it. Well, at least the lady was entertaining.

"No, I think you've led me around in circles enough for one evening." He decided to give credence to half her suggestions. "I'll ask Hagen to nose around, see what he can find out about MacFarland's dealings in the last few days."

Obviously he refused to believe that Hagen might have had something to do with stealing the statue. Maybe he was right, Elizabeth thought. Maybe the man was blameless. At the very least, Williams showed her that he had a loyal streak, which spoke well of him.

She gave him another suggestion. "You could start by seeing how much the statue is insured for."

Wrapped up in concern for his reputation, Cole had to admit that the monetary aspect of the theft had never even occurred to him. Now that he did, he immediately dismissed that as a motive. "You think MacFarland did it for the money?"

What was that old song from the twenties? Something about the rich getting richer and the poor getting poorer, Elizabeth recalled. It wasn't only the poor who liked money. "Doesn't hurt."

"Do you know how much the man's worth?"

She didn't particularly care for the dismissive tone of his laugh. Just because he was altruistic didn't mean anyone else was. "The rich never say no to money. Besides, it would be icing on the cake, wouldn't you think? Throwing mud on your reputation for pulling a switch and getting a nice insurance check on top of that?"

Cole was big enough to concede the possibility. "You might have a point."

Score two for the home team, she congratulated herself. "I always do."

"Have you had dinner?"

As if on cue, she felt her stomach rumbling. Her smile was self-deprecating and he caught himself staring at her mouth again as she said, "No."

He needed to place the length of a table between them—maybe even a football field—before he was tempted to take this relationship out of the professional realm altogether. Before? Hell, he was already tempted almost beyond human endurance. "Andre makes a mean crepe," he told her almost in self-defense.

"Andre?" she inquired.

He nodded. "My chef."

She inclined her head, a smile playing on her lips as if she was indulging him. "Of course."

He caught himself before he ran his tongue along the outline of his lips, to see if he could still taste her from last night. There was a hunger building in him that was elbowing its way past common sense. "Anything in particular you want in your crepes?"

She turned her face up to his. "Surprise me," she breathed.

Cole felt as if his heart had just stopped. And maybe, just for a moment, it did. "I'm not sure if that's possible."

Hours later, he paced around in his massive bedroom. Sleep refused to come. He had no doubt that it had something to do with the fact that Elizabeth Caldwell was only a few doors down the hall. Twice he'd caught himself going to her room with some fabricated excuse on his lips. To anyone else, he knew it would have sounded legitimate, but he knew better. And so would she.

So he remained in his room, contemplating going to sleep, knowing that it was all but futile.

Finally, because he wanted to feel as if he was accomplishing something, he'd put in a few calls to some of his overseas offices, catching up with a flow of work that never seemed to be stemmed.

His last call was to Hagen. Despite the late hour, the investigator answered on the first ring and sounded completely awake. As far as Cole knew, the man never slept.

Cole got right down to business. His request, however, seemed to take Hagen by surprise. "Say again," he remarked.

"You heard me," said Cole. "See if you can pick up anything from MacFarland's camp. Find out if anyone knows about the missing statue. If Mac-Farland's behind the theft, then he was less than happy about seeing the fake last night. That means he'd be in a foul mood right about now. He's not the kind to keep it to himself. MacFarland's taking it out on somebody and that somebody might be talking.''

"What about the girl?" Hagen wanted to know.

Yes, thought Cole. *What about the girl—or woman, as it were, because she's one hell of a prime example of one.* Cole kept his thoughts to himself. "Never mind about the girl. Leave that to me for the time being."

There was a long pause on the other end of the line. "Think that's wise, Mr. Williams? You might be a little too close to the source."

This was new, Cole thought. Hagen had never questioned him before. "Thanks for the concern, but I think I can handle one small woman."

"Isn't that what Marc Antony said about Cleopatra just before the roof caved in?"

Hagen's laugh got under his skin. "Call me back when you've got something to report," Cole instructed brusquely.

"And if there's nothing to report?"

"Call back with that, too." He ended the call and hung up the phone.

Cole paused a moment to rein in the temper he'd come close to losing. There was no denying that the woman who was currently sleeping two doors down from him had planted more than a couple of seeds of doubt in his mind. Doubts about her, doubts about himself and doubts about Hagen. Damn it, that shouldn't be. Hagen was one of the few people he felt he could rely on. The man had come to him with an excellent reputation. He'd all but guaranteed results.

Granted, he'd bought Hagen's loyalty, but integrity was something that was inherent and he felt confident that Hagen had it.

At least, he was pretty confident....

That was what this Gypsy had done to him. Shaken up his confidence, made him unsure. Unsure about his own abilities to read people. Was he wrong about Hagen? Could the man have been bought? It would explain a lot—

No, damn it, he'd known Hagen for years. He'd known her for hours. And all he knew about her was that she could bypass security systems and bend in ways the good Lord had never intended people to bend. Nothing else. Not much to go on.

And, oh yes, she could make the earth move when she kissed you.

That still didn't make it much of a résumé, certainly not one that should have caused him to have doubts about more trusted, tried and true employees.

And yet...

He blew out a breath and scrubbed his hand over his face. He was just tired and with that came an indecision, a vacillation he wasn't accustomed to. What he needed was a good night's sleep.

Or half a night's sleep, he amended, glancing at the clock on his nightstand.

Cole dropped facedown on his bed. He was wearing a pair of faded, comfortable and frayed old jeans, his sleeping apparel of choice since he was a teenager. He wore no shirt or pajama top, preferring to allow his skin to breathe.

Shutting his eyes, he concentrated on sleep.

Suddenly, a noise penetrated the silence in the room. Cole jerked his head in the direction of the sound. Screams.

Someone was screaming.

It took him less than a second to bound off his bed and reach the hallway. Once there, he oriented himself to the source of the screams.

They were coming from Elizabeth's room.

Cole ran to her door, then stopped. He heard it again. "Elizabeth?"

She gave no answer. Cole tried the doorknob, expecting to find it locked.

It gave.

Elizabeth didn't recognize the place at first. Only that it made her feel small.

Slowly, the realization came to her that it was a nursery. Her nursery.

Vague memories returned. She remembered being here, seeing life from the inside of a crib. Her earliest memories, when she'd attempted to retrace them, had formed at eighteen months.

They'd centered around her mother.

Her mother, looking down at her, smiling that sad smile of hers. Even when she was happy, she was sad, as if there was something weighing heavily on her heart. Something she tried to shield her children from.

Elizabeth felt tears welling up in her throat.

The familiar scent drifted to her, filling her senses. Her mother's scent. Gardenias.

And then she saw her. Saw her mother. Saw the storm of black hair, the small, trim figure, the gentle hands. She heard the lullaby. The tears went past her throat to her eyes.

Her mother was singing.

Singing to a baby. Her? No, not her, another baby. A different baby. She wasn't a baby; she was watching all of this. And no one saw her.

Her mother was looking down into a crib. The middle crib.

Slowly, Elizabeth became more and more aware of the surrounding area. There were three cribs lined up end to end against the wall. Her mother was standing at the center crib. Talking to the baby.

"Everything's going to be all right, my darlings. Nothing and no one will ever harm you, I promise."

Then, as Elizabeth watched, she saw another woman step out of the shadows. The other woman looked so much like her mother, but it wasn't. It was someone else. Someone her mother was talking to in another language.

Elizabeth strained to hear. Words floated to her. Foreign words she understood even though she knew she couldn't.

"Swear to me you will protect them, Magdalena.

On our mother's grave, swear,'' she heard her mother plead. "I have no one to trust but you."

"I swear," the woman promised.

And then, suddenly, the cribs were empty. The other woman was gone. Her mother was gone.

"Mama?" Elizabeth cried. "Mama, where are you?"

Panic ate away at her.

She wasn't in the nursery any longer. She was running through the house. She could hear the sound of raised voices. Arguing. The sound escalated, growing louder and louder. It echoed throughout the house.

In her head.

A deep male voice drowned out her mother's.

"What have you done with them, you bitch?! Where *are* they?" he demanded over and over again.

There was no answer. Only screams. And then there was darkness all around her.

She was in a closet. The closet Anthony had pushed all of them into. The one he told her and Dani to stay in even as he slipped out.

Except that he wasn't there.

Dani wasn't there.

She was alone in the darkness and it was all around her. Frightened, Elizabeth felt around the smooth walls, trying desperately to find the doorknob.

She couldn't find it.

Couldn't get out to see what was happening.

And then she started screaming. Surely if she

screamed, someone would hear her, someone would come and rescue her and her mommy.

Someone.

But there was only darkness. And no way out.

From the distance, a voice called out to her. Called out her name. She cowered, afraid. But then she realized it wasn't her father's voice. The voice belonged to someone else.

It was deep. Comforting.

Was it a trick?

Elizabeth felt someone taking hold of her, closing his arms around her. Her father? Was he going to kill her, too? Kill her as he'd killed her mother?

Panic infused itself through her veins. She balled up her fists and began beating at the arms, trying to break free. It did no good.

"Shh, you're all right, Elizabeth, you're all right. It was just a nightmare. Just a nightmare."

The voice was familiar, safe. But her mind was having trouble making the transition from sleep to wakefulness. Slowly, it dawned on her that she was shaking. And that someone was holding her. Struggling, she tried to pull herself together.

The need for independence triumphed over the need for reassurance.

Pushing him back, she dragged air into her lungs. Once, twice, until she could stop trembling. Only then did she open her eyes to see Cole. Only then did she trust her voice to ask, "What happened?"

"You were screaming. I guess you had a nightmare,'' he said. ''Want to tell me about it? Sometimes it helps.''

But even as Elizabeth opened her mouth, she could feel everything she'd just seen and felt fading just out of reach. The experience had felt so vivid, been so clear only seconds ago, and now she wasn't sure what it had been about, or why she'd screamed.

And why the fear hung over her so heavily, as if something dire had happened.

Or would happen.

She looked at him. Did it have to do with Cole? Was something warning her to back off? She didn't know. The harder she tried to remember what she'd dreamed, the more it eluded her, tearing at her fingers like so many gossamer webs spun by tiny spiders.

Elizabeth pressed her lips together and shook her head. ''I can't remember.''

''Must have really been bad,'' he commented. In her place, he would have wanted to be left alone, so he rose to his feet. ''Well, you know where to find me if you remember what you dreamed about, or if you just want to talk….''

He let the statement hang there.

Cole was almost at the door when he heard her. ''Don't go.''

To say that the request surprised him was putting it mildly.

He turned around to look at her. She was still in bed, her hair hanging over her face, wearing an old football jersey. A memento from a past lover? He couldn't help wondering. She didn't look like a sexy seductress now. She looked like a young woman who'd been frightened half to death.

He felt himself softening again as a protectiveness pushed forward in his chest. Cole crossed back to the bed. "What?"

"I—I don't want to be alone right now." Elizabeth raised her eyes to his, a silent entreaty there. "Would you mind?"

"No," he told her quietly, "I don't mind."

Cole shut the door.

Chapter 7

Turning from the door, Cole looked at Elizabeth for a long moment.

And then, because it was safer, he crossed to the chair instead of sitting down on the bed the way he'd done before. Elizabeth looked far too vulnerable and he was feeling things that were far too unstable to be properly harnessed if he was in close proximity to her again.

Common sense, however, didn't really cut down on the longing.

The silence in the room grew too loud. "You've had these nightmares before?" he asked.

Elizabeth nodded her head before she could think through the possible consequences of what she was admitting. She was unwittingly giving him an insight into her life.

But she wasn't thinking clearly yet. The effects of the dream still weighed her down. The horror of the nightmare was far too vivid, even if the dream no longer was.

All she could remember now was that it had something to do with her mother.

She had only distant memories of her mother and a warm feeling whenever she thought of the woman. Certain scents, certain sounds brought her mother back to her. Whenever she detected the fragrance of gardenias, or heard a wild, gypsy song, the kind her mother used to play on the stereo for hours on end, her mind instantly conjured memories of her mother.

But the violent death that had taken her mother from her, from her and Danielle and Anthony, had cast a pall over her dreams.

When she said nothing in response, Cole ventured a guess. "Was the nightmare about getting caught?"

"What?" Elizabeth blinked, coming around. Replaying his question in her mind, she was quick to pull herself out of the vacuum she'd descended into. "Oh, no. I don't do anything illegal."

Obviously the woman had a very broad definition of the word *illegal*. He felt a smile playing on his lips. "What did you call last night at the gallery?"

Good, safe ground. She could handle this far better than she could endure questions about what she'd been dreaming.

"Bending rules, not breaking them. I told you, all I wanted to do was find out if I was right about the statue, nothing more."

He still wasn't convinced that he wasn't dealing with a gorgeous version of a glorified con artist. "And your regular line of business…"

"Keeps me within the law, if only a shade," she added with what might have been able to pass as a smile. Slowly coming around, Elizabeth dragged her hand through her tangled hair, aware that Cole was watching her every move, making her feel extremely female and very conscious of the fact that she wasn't wearing anything at all beneath her jersey. Her body tingled and she ignored it. "I'm sorry if I woke you."

It was hard keeping his eyes on just her face. Hard to keep his mind on professional expectations and away from private ones.

"I wasn't asleep."

Turning her head, Elizabeth glanced at the clock on the nightstand. It was past two o'clock. "You keep hours like a bat?"

The comparison amused him. It was far from flattering, but he'd had his fill of people who flattered and pandered to him. He appreciated her genuineness. "When the bat has a lot on its mind, yes."

"This thing with the statue is really bothering you, isn't it?" She saw his amused expression. "Dumb question, huh?"

He inclined his head. "Didn't think you were capable of asking those."

She shrugged and the neckline of the jersey drooped toward one shoulder. "I'm not at my best half asleep."

It was time to get going, Cole told himself, before

he couldn't make himself leave. He rose to his feet, his eyes still on hers.

"I have a feeling that you underestimate yourself, Gypsy."

The moment lingered between them. Elizabeth could feel her heart racing again, far more pleasurably than it had in the middle of the web of dreams she'd just emerged from. Very slowly she took a deep breath, then just as slowly blew it out.

She couldn't afford to get involved with this man right now, not when her feelings were all scrambled and tossed about, raw from the dream she could no longer reconstruct. She needed to have her wits about her when and if she and Cole were ever going to come together. She needed to come in from a position of strength, not the neediness she felt right now.

"Maybe you're right," she admitted. "I've kept you long enough. Thanks for coming to my rescue."

"Any time."

After opening the door, Cole slipped out of the room, knowing it was for the best, even if his body was less than happy with the outcome. He found himself wanting her a little too much and that wasn't good. Not because he hadn't a clue about who she really was, other than the information she'd volunteered, but because he knew the kind of image he cast. To the public at large, he was a walking dollar sign. And money, to most people, was everything. He had no reason to think that Elizabeth Caldwell was any different from the rest. When they made love—and he knew it was inevitable—the time would be of his choosing. It would be out of desire and curiosity, not need, the way he felt now.

He returned to his room, wondering if there was any point in trying to get in three hours of sleep before he had to get up.

Jeremy Solienti hung up the telephone in his den and shifted in his chair to find Anthony standing in his doorway.

Perfect timing, the man thought.

He leaned back, beckoning Anthony in. After a beat, the latter pushed off the doorframe and came in. He dropped into the chair farthest from the desk and gave every indication that he was ready to regain his feet at any second.

Jeremy was accustomed to Anthony's ways. Very little caught him by surprise. "You look like someone ran over you twice and then backed up over your body one more time just for good measure. What's the matter, boy?"

Balancing his chair back on its two hind legs, Anthony Caldwell shoved his hands into his pockets, just barely curtailing a surly response that would have told Jeremy Solienti what he could do with his assessment. Dressed all in black and scowling, Elizabeth's brother gave the impression of a rogue rain cloud looking for somewhere to cast a scourge.

Jeremy's voice broke into Anthony's deep thoughts. "Something wrong with the job?"

"No, the job's finished. I wrapped it up yesterday." That was what had prompted him to stop by the house. To tell Jeremy that his client was reunited with the property that had been in questionable hands.

"Good, because I just got another one. Should be a piece of cake for you." Saying that, Jeremy paused. He had no children of his own, had never seen the need for any. But over the years, changes had occurred. He'd come to think of the three urchins he'd taken under his wing as his children. Even though Dani was now in parts unknown and Elizabeth had decided to take a breather, they were still his "kids" and would always remain that way. "If it's not the job, what is it?"

"Elizabeth's gone." Grinding the words out, Anthony rose to his feet, restless.

"Yes, I know."

"You know?" Anthony turned on the man, surprised. The blowup between his sister and him had happened several days ago and he'd said nothing, had completed the job himself when she'd abruptly taken herself off it. And all the while, Jeremy had known. The fact irritated him almost beyond belief. "You know where she is?"

Despite his anger over his sister's position, he'd been trying to connect with Elizabeth to no avail. It wasn't as if they could read each other's minds, but if they concentrated, communication of a sort was possible. At the very least, there was a feeling, a connection that allowed each to know what the other was feeling. But all of his efforts had yielded nothing, which only made him angrier. And more worried.

He didn't suffer worry well.

Anthony's scowl deepened. "Why the hell didn't you say something?"

Jeremy saw the escalating temper. He was quick to set the young man straight before an eruption occurred. "I know Elizabeth's taken off on a vacation. And that the two of you had it out just before she left. I don't, however, know where she is at the moment."

The furrows in Anthony's forehead deepened. "Then she might not be all right."

Jeremy shook his head. Anthony was way too overprotective. He'd seen it at the start, that day when they'd met, when Dani had picked his pocket. When he'd caught her hand, Anthony had come out of nowhere, ready to beat him within an inch of his life because he'd come near his sister. Eighteen years later not much had changed.

"She's not a six-week-old puppy wandering around in the wilderness, Anthony. She's a thirty-one-year-old woman with one hell of a gift. Don't worry." He waved away the concern. "She's fine."

"How do you know that?" Anthony demanded hotly, frustration clawing at him. He hated not being in control, hated not knowing. His world had been yanked away from him once, and he wasn't ever going to allow that to happen again. The only way to prevent it from happening was to maintain strict control over everything that mattered to him. "How do you know that when I don't know?"

"Maybe you're too close," Jeremy pointed out. "And maybe you don't have enough faith in her."

He looked at the young man with affection that surprised even him at times. "Your problem, Anthony, is that you've never learned how to relax, how to let things go. Maybe that's why Dani left when she did. She couldn't live life by committee with you being chairman of the board."

Anthony fisted the hands that were still shoved in his pockets. It wasn't easy hanging on to his temper, but he was trying.

"Look, old man—"

Jeremy cut him off, his voice gentle but firm. "I am looking. And I'm seeing a great deal more than you are. You can't always be the big protector, Anthony. Sometimes people have to fall down a few times in order to walk on their own. All Elizabeth wants is to be able to walk on her own."

Anthony looked at the old man sharply. "She told you?"

Jeremy shook his head. "She didn't have to. It's in my best interest to be able to make the right call while observing people. And I've known the two of you for a very long time."

Enough about this, Jeremy thought. Nothing would be settled today. Anthony was too pigheaded to concede all at once. Better they should tend to business. Maybe that would even distract Anthony.

Jeremy handed him a single sheet of paper. He'd written out the details of what their new client wanted done. "This is the new job."

Still fuming, Anthony glanced at the sheet. His

eyes narrowed as he looked up at Jeremy. "You want me to break into a laboratory and steal disks?"

"Our client maintains that they're his disks and that they were stolen from him."

Industrial espionage. Some of their best clients revolved in those worlds. "What's on them?"

"Data that he collected over the years while conducting some kind of experiments." Jeremy shrugged carelessly. "He looked a little like a mad scientist when he came to me, but the pay is very, very good."

"How good?"

Instead of telling him, Jeremy wrote the figure down on another sheet of paper, then pushed it across the desk toward Anthony.

Anthony read the sum and whistled.

"That good," he muttered, then raised his eyes back up to Jeremy's face. He knew the stakes were high when it came to industrial espionage, but judging from the money, this was head and shoulders above even that. "Why so much?"

"The guy claims it's his life's work." Jeremy shrugged again. "Ours isn't to ask questions, just to deliver. As long as the price is right," he added with a smile. Business had been very good lately. Even with Dani gone, his young protégés had exceeded all of his expectations.

"And you're sure these disks are his?" Anthony queried.

Jeremy's eyes met his for a long moment. "He says they are. That's enough for us."

Rule of thumb was that asking the client too many

questions left them wide open to a host of problems and possible legal issues down the line. "Don't ask, don't tell" had become their motto. Theirs wasn't to question, just to get in and out as fast as possible.

Anthony folded what amounted to a work order and placed the sheet into his back pocket. Vague curiosity prompted him to ask, "So what's this guy's name?"

"Titan."

That seemed like an odd name for a person, Anthony thought. It was more like something that belonged to a company logo. "Titan what?"

Jeremy spread his hands wide. "That's all he'd tell me. Just Titan."

"Titan," Anthony repeated. Egos were a driving force in their business. Anthony laughed shortly. There was no mirth in the sound. "Like one of the gods?"

Jeremy nodded. The phone was ringing again. More business? Mentally, he rubbed his hands together. Maybe he'd have to find Elizabeth and get her to cut her vacation short. "He certainly thought he was. Now go." He waved him out. "Do me proud."

"Yes, Papa," Anthony quipped as he left.

Elizabeth didn't sleep very much. Maybe it was fear that kept her from drifting off. Maybe it was the distinct scent of his cologne that insisted on lingering in the room long after Cole had left it.

Whatever the reason, she got no more rest that night. She gave up all attempts at six o'clock, rose and got ready. There was a full day of work ahead of her and trails to follow before they got cold.

Through connections and skills that had been honed to a fine point over the years, she began to pull pieces of the puzzle together. Granted her starting point was a theory, but it was a theory she was damn confident of, even if the evidence was circumstantial. Her feeling that MacFarland was behind the theft was unshakable.

Proceeding from there, she managed to get information about the insurance policy MacFarland carried on his artwork. The most heavily insured piece in his collection was *Venus Smiling.*

Big surprise there, she thought as she made her notes.

"And the thing that you might find interesting," she told Cole later that day when she came to his office with an update, "is that he'd recently had the amount on that piece raised from one to two million dollars."

She'd surprised him, coming into his office with a protesting Ms. Witherspoon in her wake. His secretary didn't appreciate being ignored or usurped. Gypsy, apparently, wasn't aware that she was doing either.

Sitting back in his chair, he'd let her make her case while he played devil's advocate. "Inflation," he countered.

With the courage of her convictions, Elizabeth stubbornly dug in. "Or planning."

Cole had to admit, she was making a good case.

He'd done a little looking into MacFarland's history himself and what she'd pointed out was true, the man had been on the board of a great many of the businesses his empire had taken over.

"Okay, he does stand to gain financially. And let's say you're right, MacFarland is out for my reputation—"

Satisfaction shone in her eyes, making her just that much more attractive. Damn, but she made it hard to keep his mind on his work.

"The picture of you being led off in cuffs would make a nice little photo for him to carry around in his wallet," she said with sarcasm.

The flippant statement brought reality back with a thud. There was no way he was going to be questioned about the statue. He could see the whole drama unfolding. MacFarland would have the statue examined once it was returned. Any appraiser worth his fee would see that it was a fake. Which would point the finger at him. "We need to find the real statue."

She nodded. "My guess is that people like MacFarland are creatures of habit. The statue, most likely, is probably where he's kept it all along. For his private viewing."

He thought of MacFarland's estate. Five acres with a sprawling, ostentatious mansion in the middle. And a great deal of security that wasn't visible to the naked eye. "The place is like a fortress. Planning on bending your way in?"

He made her sound as if she were a comic book superhero instead of a resourceful woman. "Maybe eventually. I was thinking of something a little more conventional to start with. Like an invitation to the party he's having next Saturday night.''

He wasn't even aware that MacFarland was having a party. Gaining access to it wouldn't be an easy matter. He looked at her suspiciously. Had she accidentally allowed something to slip?

''You know him?''

She shook her head, sporting a smile that would have done Mona Lisa proud had she thought to wear it first on her lips. ''Not yet, but I will after you introduce me to him at your party.''

Obviously he'd missed something here. ''What party?'' he wanted to know.

Spreading her hands on his desk, she leaned over it until her face was close to his. She tried very hard not to draw in the scent of his cologne. It would only scramble her thoughts. Remind her that as far as any kind of intimate interaction went, she was in way over her head.

''The small, intimate one you're going to throw tomorrow night. Just him and a few of your closer associates.'' Her smile rose into her eyes. It was fascinating to watch. ''And me. The woman you can't take your eyes off.'' She laughed. The sound tickled him. ''If I'm right about this man, he wants anything you want, just for spite. I get him to invite me to the party and the rest will be easy.''

''You're that confident.''

''Success is built on confidence.'' She straightened again, growing practical, concentrating on what she knew. "And preparation. I'll need the layout of his house."

He laughed at her. "Just like that."

She heard the doubt and didn't let it stop her. "Every house has a builder." And with that, she was in the doorway again, ready to take flight. "Now let me do my work. You start arranging for the party."

He had a curve to throw her. "What if he doesn't come?"

"Oh, he'll come, all right," she told him. There was no doubt in her voice. "He wouldn't pass up anything in his honor."

The two men had entered into a vast merger together, but neither had ever consciously entered the other's intimate social circles. Given a choice, Cole would rather keep it that way.

"And why would I—"

"To thank him for lending you the statue. The irony of it will be too much for him to pass up." She winked. "Trust me."

And then she was gone, leaving the effect of her wink to linger over him. To make his gut tighten and his mind wander.

Trust me.

That was exactly what he was doing and Cole couldn't help wondering if he was going to regret it in the long run.

Chapter 8

"So, how do I look?"

When he turned around in the living room, Cole saw her walking down the stairs toward him. Elizabeth stopped at the bottom of the stairs and twirled before him, a vision in blue. Her dress clung to her curves the way he longed to. It was five minutes to the hour and MacFarland and the other five guests he'd invited were due within the heartbeat.

Having just poured two glasses of wine, he handed one to her. And discovered that he wanted more than just a moment alone with her.

"Too beautiful to waste on the likes of Jonathan MacFarland."

She smiled that smile at him, the one that could disarm an entire army battalion at fifty paces. "Good, that's exactly how I wanted to look."

He paused, openly studying her. There was so much he didn't know about her, so many blank spaces that hadn't been filled.

"You've done this before. Played con games," he clarified when she looked at him quizzically. "Haven't you?"

The doorbell rang just then, saving her.

Flashing a smile, she patted Cole's arm. He knew she was dismissing the question. "Just let me do my job," she whispered as his housekeeper, Cummings, went to answer the door.

From the very first moment the other man laid eyes on her, Cole could see that Jonathan MacFarland wanted Elizabeth. Wanted her not just because she was the most beautiful woman in the room, but because MacFarland thought that she belonged to him.

Elizabeth was right, Cole thought. The rivalry that MacFarland perceived between them went deep. And it seemed to be all-consuming for the man.

Well, they'd set it up this way, hadn't they? Set it up so that MacFarland would be drawn to her and would act upon that attraction.

Cole had introduced her to MacFarland and the others simply as Elizabeth, leaving her last name out of it. Creating an aura of mystery about her. When it came his turn to meet her, MacFarland had held Elizabeth's hand a little longer than was necessary, as if he was already thinking about sampling her.

Something twisted within Cole's gut, and it took

more effort than he would have thought to keep his calm exterior in place.

His smile felt a little tight around the edges as he told MacFarland, "I guess I have you to thank for meeting Elizabeth."

MacFarland looked at him blankly, his wide, florid face a puzzled roadmap. Shifting his eyes back to her, he directed his question to Elizabeth. "Oh? And how's that?"

"We met at the gallery opening the other night. In front of your beautiful sculpture," she told him. "*Venus Smiling.* I came expressly to see it."

MacFarland's small, piglike brown eyes devoured her. More guests were arriving behind him. MacFarland took the opportunity to draw her away from the man he considered his rival in everything, his equal in nothing.

"Are you interested in art?" MacFarland posed seductively.

It took absolutely no effort to infuse enthusiasm in her voice. "I adore it. Art has always been one of the passions of my life."

She saw delight enter the brown orbs. "Then you must come to my home. I've a great many pieces of art that just might interest you." His eyes slid down to her neckline and the hint of cleavage that was detectable there. "I'm a very renowned collector."

"Yes, I know," she murmured, deliberately looking up into his eyes as if he were the only man in the room, or at the very least, the most fascinating.

From across the room, Cole observed her in action.

He had to admit that the web she was spinning around MacFarland was a thing of beauty. He didn't have to hear the words to know that she was playing the man like a pro. Body language told him what he wanted to know.

She wasn't being too eager, just enough to place the bait out in the water and then wait for him to take it. MacFarland, so full of pride, so full of himself, took no notice that there was a hook in his mouth and that he was being reeled in ever so slowly.

He looked as if he sincerely believed that all the moves being executed were his.

Cole didn't waste any energy being sorry for the other man. He was struggling to bank down a completely new sensation before it overtook him.

Right after dinner, MacFarland focused his attention on Elizabeth to the exclusion of everyone else. He maneuvered her into a corner in order to monopolize her. Each time Cole looked they seemed to be deep in conversation. As he played host to the other guests he'd invited for the evening, he attempted to ignore the sound of Elizabeth's soft, melodic laughter as it reached him time and again. He told himself that she was only carrying out the plan they'd agreed on.

Or she had, he amended. Playing up to the overweight, opinionated billionaire had been strictly her idea.

As he struggled to keep his mind on the conversation, Cole couldn't help wondering if it was MacFarland who was the one being played. What if she was actually in on this with him and the two of them were playing Cole instead? Maybe they were leading him down a darkened trail for some purpose that hadn't yet occurred to him.

Maybe he was being set up and he didn't know it.

He felt someone's hand on his shoulder. Coming around, he found himself looking into the concerned face of one of his oldest friends, Jeff Jackson. "Cole, are you all right?"

Cole flushed. He was usually better than this at keeping his thoughts from registering on his face. "Sorry." He shrugged carelessly. "Just preoccupied."

Jeff looked over his shoulder in Elizabeth's direction.

"Yes, and I can see why. She is beautiful." He lowered his voice just a trifle. "Looks like Mac-Farland wants to add her to his collection."

Cole realized that if he didn't loosen his hold on the stem of his glass, it was going to snap. He took a breath before forcing an easygoing smile he didn't feel.

"He can try."

Closing the door as the last guest left, Cole turned around. He felt testy and he knew it. Something strange and unsettling was going on inside him. He supposed if he analyzed it closely, he might say that it was jealousy. Never having experienced it before, he wasn't sure.

He'd wanted to rip Jonathan MacFarland's hand off

instead of shake it when he'd taken his leave. Especially after the man had raised Elizabeth's hand to his lips and kissed it.

"Don't forget tomorrow," he'd said to her as if he already owned her, body and soul, but was too well-mannered to say so.

And for her part, Elizabeth had smiled up into his wide face and promised, "I won't."

"Tomorrow?" Cole finally asked as he came away from the door.

She saw the odd look on Cole's face. Like a volcano on the verge of erupting. But why? Wasn't this what the whole evening had been about? To gain MacFarland's confidence? "He's invited me over for dinner. To see his collections," she added when Cole said nothing.

His expression darkened. "They used to call it etchings," he bit off, looking at her. "That was a euphemism for—"

She cut him off. "I know what it was a euphemism for." Did he think she was some innocent babe? Damn it, why was he treating her the way Anthony always had? It was the last thing she wanted or needed. "But I just intend to see as much of his collection as he'll allow me to. Nothing else," she underscored. "Except to do a little planting," she added with a smile.

Drifting over to the den, she mentally went over her own plan, then said aloud, "I'll probably need three or four cameras." She'd seen the schematics of the mansion and in order to penetrate the surveillance system and hack into its monitors, she was going to need to use more than one point of access.

After pouring himself a whiskey, neat, Cole threw it down, then blew out a breath, trying to harness the impatience, the frustration he felt. Whether she needed three or three hundred cameras didn't matter. Technology wasn't the problem. He had easy access to state-of-the-art equipment, some of which was currently housed within his desk.

No, the problem went far deeper than the need for any electronic device. And it bothered him on a great many levels.

He debated pouring another whiskey, then decided against it. A fuzzy mind was not the answer.

Cole set his glass down. "He looked really taken with you."

There was an odd tone in his voice, Elizabeth noted, and she struggled to get a handle on it. But Cole Williams was not the easiest man to read.

"That was the plan, wasn't it? To get MacFarland 'taken' with me." Elizabeth found that she rather liked the old-fashioned term as she rolled it around on her tongue.

"Yes," Cole told her tersely. Because the temptation to numb his thoughts was becoming progressively more urgent, he shoved his hands into his pockets and crossed to the other side of the room.

She stayed where she was, watching him, trying to untangle the puzzle that was Cole Williams. "Then you should be very happy."

"I am," he snapped at her.

Since he wouldn't come to her, she crossed to him. Elizabeth peered up into his face, pretending to examine his expression. "You don't look like a man who's very happy."

No, he wasn't, he thought. He was a man who wasn't comfortable about what he was experiencing. Something that seemed to be out of his control, which made it that much worse because he was determined to be in control always. That way there were no surprises, no sudden upsets. "I just don't like feeding sheep to lions."

Meaning her. Elizabeth raised her chin defensively. "I'm hardly a sheep."

Damn it, didn't she understand? She was out of her element here. "You are to MacFarland. The way he was looking at you—"

She cocked her head, looking at Cole. Waiting. "Yes?"

Huffing, he moved around Elizabeth. Right now he needed distance between them. Just having her in front of him was clouding his thoughts, heating his blood. The thought of MacFarland even so much as touching her enraged him.

"He was already dissecting you and having you for lunch."

Yes, no doubt about it, Elizabeth thought, Cole was beginning to sound just like Anthony. All right, so she didn't look like a woman who made her living wrestling alligators, but that didn't mean she could be snapped in two like a twig, either. She'd taken care of herself in more than one situation.

"I'm not that digestible," she assured him, "and I'm not that easily devoured." Because she found herself talking to his back, she moved around to face him. "Trust me, you underestimate me."

He didn't like the images he was getting. Mac-Farland was going to want to have her the second she walked across his threshold. "You're going to be alone with him in that big house."

She struggled to keep her grin from her lips. Williams was jealous. Wow, who would have thought it? "He has servants."

"Who are paid to look the other way," he pointed out heatedly.

She placed her hand on his arm, her voice soothing. "Look, this is all part of the plan. We need to be sure that we're right about this. I go and plant a few tiny cameras around his lovely barn of a mansion. They hook up into his main surveillance cameras and maybe, if we're lucky, we can see or hear a few things before the big party next Saturday so we can get our hands on the statue before he figuratively gets his hands on you."

That was something else that wasn't working for him. "MacFarland isn't just going to let you play pin the camera wherever you want to."

"No," she agreed lightly. "But a lady has to powder her nose sometime. Maybe even a few times if she's been drinking." She second-guessed the look in his eyes. "Don't worry, I'll make sure to subtly pour the drinks out. I don't plan to get the slightest bit tipsy around MacFarland."

All right, so maybe she could hold her own against the man. But Cole had another concern to address. "They'll see you planting the cameras."

He'd shown her the cameras she was going to be using earlier. "They're hardly larger than micro-chips."

She was missing the point, he thought, annoyance vying for control of him. "You still have to place them where they won't be seen, which means getting on your knees, or doing something out of the ordinary that's bound to make red flags go up."

They'd already decided that they needed to plant several cameras in strategic places in order to hack into the main surveillance system at the mansion. Once that was accomplished, if the Rodin statue was on the premises somewhere, they would be able to locate it and set plans in motion to remove it back to the gallery.

"It doesn't matter how beautiful you are," Cole told her. "If MacFarland finds out that you're trying to get back the statue so that I can hand it over to him, you're a dead woman."

The smile on her lips annoyed him even further. "Figuratively speaking?" she asked playfully.

"Maybe not." This wasn't a game, damn it, but she was treating it as one. "Forget it, it's a bad plan."

"It's a very good plan." The look on his face told her that he was calling it off. And it was his show. But suddenly she wasn't willing to let him do that. Not if it was because he was worried about her. Why did all the men in her life think she was so incompetent? ''What about your reputation?''

He took hold of her shoulders. The thought of shaking some sense into her head crossed his mind. ''I'm not about to keep my reputation at the risk of having someone hurt. It's too high a price.''

Her mouth would have fallen open if she hadn't exercised extreme control over her muscles. Williams was being sincere. He was willing to risk having his reputation challenged because he didn't want to take a chance on getting her hurt or worse.

Elizabeth looked at him for a long moment, debating her next step. Very few people knew what she was actually capable of. Mentally, she ticked them off. There was Dani and Anthony, of course, and Jeremy. That was all. A very small circle of confidants. She'd always been careful not to let anyone else see what she could do.

Maybe it was time to widen the circle by one.

She needed one more piece of information before she made up her mind. Watching his face carefully, confident she could catch him in a lie if it came to that, she asked, ''Are you easily freaked out?''

He narrowed his brow. ''No. Why?''

She didn't answer. Instead, she made a request. ''Get out one of those cameras.''

He had no idea where this was going, but he took one of the cameras out of the center desk drawer and placed it on top of the desk. ''Okay, now what?''

Instead of picking it up, she left it there. ''Where do you want it?''

"What?" He didn't particularly want the camera anywhere. It was to be planted in MacFarland's mansion, not here.

"Pick a place," she told him evenly. "Where do you want me to put the camera?"

Cole had no idea what she was trying to accomplish. All he knew was that he felt annoyed and frustrated. There were feelings bouncing around inside him, colliding, crashing, leaving him bewildered and shell-shocked, and he didn't like it one damn bit. He waved a hand dismissively around the area. "I don't know." Because she continued looking at him expectantly, he finally said, "Put it on top of the computer."

"All right."

Elizabeth took in a deep cleansing breath, then let it out. She made no move, held her body rigid, her eyes sealed to the camera. She really didn't need to look at it. Strict concentration on the small chip was the actual key to moving it, but it helped her focus if she stared and she wanted this over with as quickly as possible. Speed, she knew, was going to be of the essence once she was inside MacFarland's house.

"I don't understand—" Cole began.

Without looking in his direction she held her hand up, silencing him.

The protest forming on his lips faded.

The chip had begun to move. On its own.

It moved slowly, as if guided by invisible fingers. Leaving the table, it rose into the air until it finally settled on top of the computer.

"Now I really don't understand," Cole whispered softly, as if afraid to disturb some unseen force within the room.

The only force in the room was standing next to him.

Hardly breathing, he drew his eyes away from the chip and looked at Elizabeth. Who the hell was she? "How did you do that?"

"I don't know," she replied quite honestly. "I just did."

Cole shook himself free of the eerie feeling that had zipped along his spine. "C'mon, there has to be some kind of trick behind it."

She looked at him with the most serious eyes he'd ever seen. "No, no trick. I've always been able to move objects."

She was playing him for a fool, he thought. What annoyed him most was that he couldn't figure out how. "Yeah, most people can, but they usually use hands. Or wires, or—"

Elizabeth slowly moved her head from side to side, negating anything he might suggest. "No 'or,'" she replied quietly.

Cole caught himself leaning against the desk, trying to steady himself. This wasn't something that he could easily accept. And yet, she'd done it. "And you've always had this ability?"

She nodded. "For as long as I can remember. I found out about it when I was very, very young." She saw that he was waiting for details. Well, she'd started this, she thought, she might as well give him a little more. "I was in my crib and there was a bottle of juice on the table. My mother was busy tending to one of the others—"

He couldn't believe he was listening to this, and yet he couldn't bring himself just to dismiss it out of hand, either. "Others?"

"I'm a triplet."

Up until this moment, he'd thought of her as being one of a kind, unique. Maybe it was because he no longer had a family of his own that he'd attributed the same set of circumstances to her. But obviously he'd been wrong. "There's more like you?"

She grinned. Did he realize there was a small note of, if not horror, then shock in his voice? "In a manner of speaking. They can do other things."

He liked to think that he had an open mind, but this was getting harder and harder to absorb. "Go on," he urged when she'd stopped.

"I was thirsty, she was busy. I remember staring at the bottle, and the next thing I knew, it was in my hands. I was eighteen months old."

That in itself sounded impossible. His earliest memory was when he was four and on the beach, playing with his sister.

"Maybe your mother handed it to you."

Elizabeth shook her head. She knew what she knew. "I remember the surprised look on my mother's face." A small smile curved her lips. "A little like the one on yours right now."

He would have accused her of lying, but he'd seen

it for himself and there was no way she could have rigged it. ''What else?''

Her eyes narrowed in confusion. ''What do you mean?''

''What else can you do?'' He enunciated the question very carefully, not at all certain he knew what to feel about the woman standing before him. ''You don't move through walls or anything like that, do you?''

She laughed as she shook her head. ''You're confusing me with the X-Men. No, I don't move through walls. I also don't grow hair and howl at the moon when it's full. There *is* a basis for telekinesis, you know.''

He knew a little something about telekinesis. ''Most of it's been proven to be fraud. Parlor tricks.''

''This is no parlor trick.'' His reluctance to believe her irritated her. ''It's how I got into the gallery that first night. I made the padlock open.''

It sounded incredible, and yet it made more sense than anything else. ''That's why the alarm didn't go off. The lock was wired so that the lightest touch, the slightest pressure against it would have caused it to go off.''

She held up her hands to underscore her point. ''No touch, no pressure. Just mind over matter.'' She looked at him for a long moment. Finally, she ventured to ask the question that had been echoing in her mind, the one that had made her keep her secret to herself even when she'd been tempted to share it. ''Horrified?''

"No, not horrified. Stunned, maybe," he admitted. He realized there was probably nothing she could do that would actually horrify him. "This is something I'm going to have to work at wrapping my mind around." As he said that, he took a step back.

He was backing away from her. No matter what he said to the contrary, he *was* horrified. Telling him had been a mistake. She'd done it to assuage his concerns and now there wasn't anything she could do to retract what she'd told him.

She gave a half shrug. "I just wanted you not to worry about me."

The fact that she could bend spoons or move microchips didn't alleviate his concerns. "This is still a dangerous game you're about to get into." He made up his mind. "You're not going in alone."

"I have to." He couldn't come in with her; that would ruin everything. "Otherwise, MacFarland'll suspect something. He'll be on his guard."

There wasn't anything she could say that would get him to change his mind. "I'm going to be nearby. I want you to carry an open cell phone on you so that if something goes wrong—"

In a way, this was rather sweet, she decided. Anthony had always ordered her around, told her what to do. Cole was being thoughtful. "You'll come riding in like the cavalry."

"Something like that."

She smiled and her eyes crinkled just a bit. "I think I might like that."

When she smiled like that, it hit him dead center

and made him forget all about being cautious. "Does it work on people?"

He was jumping around again. "Does what work on people?"

"Your talent, your gift, your—" At a loss, he waved his hand. "Whatever you call it."

She grinned. "I call it Max," she teased. Actually, beyond telekinesis, she'd never really referred to it as anything in particular. Just her way. "And I've never tried to move anything that was alive."

"Probably wouldn't have to," he speculated. He could feel her pull even as he stood there. "You can make them come to you without having to exercise mind control over them."

She didn't want him getting the wrong idea. "It's not mind control."

"Oh, I don't know about that." Lightly, he combed his fingers through her hair. He could feel himself becoming aroused. "You keep attracting me—"

She could feel the air standing still in her lungs again. He kept having that effect on her. "Ever think that just might be one of those things that happen between men and women?"

"Crossed my mind." Cole ran the back of his knuckle slowly along her cheek. The brush of her skin against his made him catch his breath. "But I'm not usually attracted to a business associate."

She smiled up at him. "First time for everything."

"Yes, you might have something there," Cole told her with a smile just before he slipped his hand into her hair again.

Tilting her head back, he brought his lips down to hers.

Movements began within him, within her, that had absolutely nothing to do with telekinesis and everything to do with the feelings between a man and a woman who found themselves utterly and hopelessly attracted to each other.

Chapter 9

He was draining her. Draining all the energy out of her body and replacing it with a need so huge, so boundless, it threatened to burst out of her and take over the entire room.

Elizabeth dug her fingertips into his shoulders, channeling the tension she felt. She tried desperately to regain some semblance of control before she just gave herself up to Cole completely without so much as an effort to hold on.

Because she wanted to.

Wanted to finally feel that dizzying rapture she'd heard called lovemaking. Beneath the carefully or-chestrated, sophisticated facade she wore, she be-lieved in every silly little love song, every romantic movie, every passage she'd ever read within a book that talked about the magic that went along with wanting someone.

Because she knew magic was real.

She felt it in her veins. How else to describe the things that she could do?

Mysterious things that defied explanation *were* possible. Magic was possible. And she wanted to feel the magic.

If only she could feel it and still somehow be in control. Because control, so newly found, meant everything to her. She wanted the power of her own independence, wanted to be the mistress of her own destiny, and this man, this feeling, this rush threatened to sweep it all away from her.

"I want you," Cole murmured against her lips as she began to draw away.

She let her eyes close as she absorbed the sensuousness of his words. If her heart beat any harder, it was going to take off on its own, break the sound barrier as it went.

Elizabeth opened her eyes and looked at him. His face was less than an inch away from hers. It took her a moment to gather herself together, to try to form words when all she wanted to do was cry, "Yes!"

"I know," she finally said, just barely succeeding in keeping the sigh from escaping.

They were standing so close, Cole could taste the words sliding along his lips. He'd left himself open, vulnerable, and that wasn't good. He'd never done that before.

And wasn't about to ever do it again.

It didn't change the fact that what he'd told her was true. He wanted her. Wanted her in the best, in the worst way.

"But?" he prodded, hearing the word silently follow the others.

She gave him the best excuse she could manage at the moment. "But I have to concentrate."

Cole tried to discern if she was being serious, or if this was her way of flirting. "You don't have to levitate me."

"No, I mean about tomorrow. I think I should get some rest." *Before I forget all about being level-headed and just jump your bones.*

That was what she was afraid of, that she was a victim of freshly unleashed hormones. There was no more Anthony to grab her by the arm and drag her away every time her interest was piqued.

And she had to remember there were consequences for every action.

Something warned her that the consequences here were far from minor. For one thing, her heart was in danger of being forever lost. Lost to a man who probably thought nothing of sleeping with a different woman every week. Carefree or not, that wasn't what she wanted. That was too few strings to satisfy her.

Cole leaned ever closer, till only a breath separated them. "Can you rest now?" he said on a whisper.

The safe, expedient thing would have been to say "yes," but it had too flippant a ring. It would have also been a lie.

Elizabeth looked at him for a long moment and finally admitted, "I don't know. It won't be easy."

No, it certainly wasn't going to be that. Urges continued to nip insistently at him. Urges he struggled to resist. Elizabeth was right and he knew it. Right because she needed her rest if she was going to be any good to him tomorrow. And if what was on the brink of happening between them happened, there'd be no rest for either of them until way into dawn.

And she was also right because if he made love with her now, while he felt this way, who knew where it would lead? Emotions could escalate, explode, and he couldn't risk that happening.

He had enough going on in his life right now without borrowing trouble.

"Yeah," he told her, taking a long step back. "Won't be easy for me, either." Turning on his heel, he walked away. "I'll see you in the morning."

And I'll see you in my dreams, she thought, knowing that there would be no rest for her, one way or another, tonight.

But if she made love with him, she'd be imprisoning her soul and she couldn't risk that. Not when freedom was so new.

"Sure you don't want to back out?"

Her nerves, newly polished and at their most alert, chafed at his question. Why didn't he give it a rest already? Instead of looking at him, Elizabeth stared at the scenery as it went by. Like Williams, Mac-Farland lived outside of Philadelphia, in the suburbs, where people pretended cities, with their grit and crowds, didn't exist.

"You've asked me that twice already," Elizabeth pointed out.

He had to concentrate to keep from gripping the steering wheel so hard his knuckles hurt. "Just want to make sure you have plenty of opportunity to change your mind."

She was dressed to kill and wired, mentally not physically. She didn't need anything negative getting in her way.

"You're not paying me to change my mind, you're paying me for results? All we have now is my gut feeling that MacFarland took the statue, and time's growing short, remember?" She didn't bother keeping the impatience out of her voice. He was beginning to treat her like a girl instead of a capable partner.

"I remember," he bit off. He didn't like feeling this degree of concern over getting something done. But what she was about to do fell outside the lines that he was accustomed to. Gray areas were for people like MacFarland, not him, and he damned the man's soul for putting him in this kind of position. "I don't need you to remind me."

"No, you need me to get the sculpture back for you," she told him cheerfully. She was warming to her task, if not to the idea of spending the evening with MacFarland. "Step one: ascertain location of target."

They were swiftly approaching the man's elaborate mansion. As the distance grew shorter, Cole's misgivings about the entire venture loomed larger. He didn't like putting anyone in harm's way, and the risk factor was something he was unsure of. What would MacFarland do if he discovered that Elizabeth wasn't his lady of the moment, but that she actually worked for him? That she was here to find out if he'd stolen his own statue? Just how ugly could MacFarland get?

For her sake, Cole didn't want to find out. "I've got a bad feeling about this."

"No, you don't," she informed him cheerfully. When she saw him scowling at her, she clarified, "You've got a nervous feeling about it. They're two very different things. Now let me do my work."

She had an annoying habit of making it sound as if he got in her way. The woman, he decided, was definitely getting under his skin and that wasn't good. "You keep saying that."

She slanted him a look. "Because you keep interfering."

He was almost at the front door. Nerves, blunt and jagged, were making themselves known. "You have your phone open?"

In response, she lifted the tiny instrument out of her purse. The instant she touched it, the light went on its display, showing him that it was on. Cole nodded his approval.

Elizabeth redeposited the phone in her clutch. Hidden beneath the cell were the three cameras she was to plant. "May I go now?"

"Yeah." But as she began to leave the vehicle, Cole caught her arm. Elizabeth looked back at him quizzically, patiently, the way a parent might look at a child. When had their positions gotten reversed? "Be careful."

Anthony had said the same words to her a million times. More. Growled them usually, like a warning. But there was something in Cole's eyes that made the words sound entirely different. Elizabeth paused, a smile slipping along her lips. She leaned back inside the car and lightly brushed them against his. "Don't worry so much. I'll find the statue."

"It's not the statue I'm worried about," Cole muttered more to himself than to her.

Elizabeth was already out of the car and hurrying up to the entrance of the mansion. He had no choice but to appear to be driving away.

Circling around to the right, Cole turned off the main path and doubled back. Driving to a more secluded area of the estate, he hid the small vehicle behind some tall, wispy shrubbery he vaguely recognized. Mr. Lei, his gardener, took great pride in his work and tried, whenever possible, to educate him about the names of the various greenery planted around his property. It appeared that Mr. Lei and MacFarland shared an affinity for Leylandi cypress.

He just hoped he and MacFarland didn't share an affinity for something else. *Too late for that,* he thought. Anyone with eyes could see that MacFarland was attracted to Elizabeth.

He took out the cell phone that was connected to Elizabeth's, made sure that the Mute function was on and placed it on the passenger seat.

Settling back in the car, Cole did something he wasn't very good at. He waited.

MacFarland greeted Elizabeth personally at the door instead of having his housekeeper bring her to him. Clasping her hand in both of his, he kissed it soundly, then tucked her arm through his as he brought her into the foyer.

The only word that came to mind as she looked around was *magnificent*. It was the kind of house that had required the expert talents of an army of decorators all working in perfect harmony. They had done it and it showed.

Everywhere she looked, there were precious works of art, either hanging on the walls or placed lovingly on pedestals. What a shame she loathed the man. She truly loved the house, Elizabeth thought.

"Would you like to see my collection before or after?"

At MacFarland's question, she raised one delicate eyebrow and turned her attention to him. "Before or after what?"

His eyes became lost in the depth of his smile. "Before or after I give you a tour of my bedroom suite."

Well, that hadn't taken any time, she remarked to herself. "You certainly are direct."

His broad shoulders rose and fell beneath the perfectly tailored suit. "There's no point in beating around the bush." His eyes met hers. "Unless it's for enhancement of the moment."

Her stomach was definitely in danger of rising up into her throat and gagging her. She forced herself to playfully run the tip of her finger along his lips, which required a measure of charity to be called beefy. "But there is a point in prolonging the moment."

He drew himself up to his full six foot four. "If you're talking about stamina—"

"No," she said softly, her voice melodious, though she wanted to gag. "I'm talking about anticipation." She indicated the decanter placed strategically on the bar beside two balloon glasses. "Take Napoleon brandy, for instance. Surely you'd rather sniff a beguiling bouquet, anticipating the way it will taste on your palate, than just throw it back like it was a cheap whiskey."

"Yes, but—"

Taking the liberty, she poured him a glass, then one for herself. It was going to be a shame to dispose of her brandy, but she wasn't about to chance a head that was in the slightest bit unclear.

"Think of me as Napoleon brandy," she prompted, handing him his glass. "Something far too rare to be tossed back quickly." Placing her lips on the glass, she pretended to take a sip, her eyes never leaving MacFarland's. She could see his desire growing. "You have to build up to it." With a heartfelt, pleased sigh, she shifted the glass to her other hand, slipped her arm through his and smiled up into his face. "Now, I would just love to see your collection before dinner."

She was good, Cole thought as he listened to Elizabeth on the other end. Again, he glanced down at the Mute button to make sure it was depressed. They couldn't afford to chance having a stray sound from his end filtering through and alerting MacFarland that she had the cell on. Jonathan MacFarland had more than his share of suspicious bones in his body and surely he'd think there was something going on.

Images that went along with their voices began to ricochet through his mind as he listened. Elizabeth grew lovelier, more desirable by the moment, and MacFarland took on the stature of a rutting pig before the tour was even half completed.

It was going to be a long night.

Cole sat in the dark, listening, growing edgier by the moment.

Now she knew exactly what it felt like to be a scarlet cape, the kind that the matador swung majestically before a charging bull, waving it in front of the beast, pulling it back at the last possible moment to avoid having the fabric caught on one of the deadly horns and shredded. That was the dance that she and MacFarland were performing. She was the cape, he was the bull.

She had managed to elude him skillfully all through the intimate dinner. It required drawing on the vast education Jeremy had drummed into her head to make endless distracting conversation. She never rejected the man's advances outright, just kept him at bay. But not so far as to make him grow angry and either send her home before she was finished, or to take what he so obviously felt was his due.

Cleverly, she kept herself out of confining corners, never allowing him to cut off her route of escape. During the course of the evening, she'd excused herself once to use the bathroom. The winding path there had allowed her to plant two of the three cameras she'd brought with her.

Dinner was over and they had done justice to the bottle of wine he'd served with it. The potted plant to her right should have been humming old drinking songs, she mused. By morning, it was going to be in serious danger of rotting. She knew it was time to beat a retreat or be served as dessert. But she still had one camera to go.

She was running out of time. MacFarland gave all the indications of a man who wanted to cap off his evening and she was the designated nightcap.

He leaned over to lightly brush her lips with his, but when he reached out to pull her against him, she managed to elude his grasp and rise to her feet.

Glancing over her shoulder at him seductively, she drifted over to the wall where one of his oldest acquisitions, a late Picasso, hung. He rose to his feet and crossed to her.

"I have heard that you have a, shall we say, more 'private' collection."

She couldn't tell by his expression if she had unnerved him, or if he'd expected her to know. "Oh, that. I only show those to my very special friends."

Meaning he wanted her to go to bed with him before she got to see anything. *No dice, fella,* she silently remarked.

"I see." With deliberate strokes, she flattened the skirt of her dress against her thighs, then looked up at him. MacFarland was all but salivating like a starving dog over a soup bone. "Well, then, how do I become one of those special—"

Elizabeth abruptly broke off her question, suddenly clutching at her stomach. Her eyes widened, registering surprise coupled with pain.

Staring at her uncertainly, MacFarland grasped her arm. "What's the matter?"

"Bathroom," was all she managed to get out.

Yanking her arm out of his hold, keeping one hand over her mouth, the other still pressed against her stomach, Elizabeth raced out of the room.

"What's the matter?" MacFarland repeated.

He saw her stop in the hallway, her hand splayed out on a table for support. But by the time he rushed over, she was back to making her way to the bathroom, her path zigzagging from one wall to the other.

"Are you ill?" he called after her.

His question was answered with the slamming of the bathroom door.

Alone in the bathroom, Elizabeth doubled over the toilet bowl, just in case he burst in, and made the appropriate retching noises. After a sufficient amount of time had lapsed, she rose to her feet again and flushed. She looked at herself in the mirror, assumed a haggard expression and threw cold water in her face to make it appear as if she was perspiring.

Satisfied that she'd achieved the look she was after, Elizabeth opened the door, then sank against the doorjamb as she looked at MacFarland.

"I'm afraid you're going to have to show me your private collection some other time." Her voice was weak, reedy. "I don't feel so good."

"You don't look all that good, either," he told her tersely, no doubt disgusted that the evening was going to end like this. MacFarland's germ phobia was well known, so she knew he wouldn't chance touching her. He picked up a phone and summoned his driver. "I'll have someone drive you home."

"As long as I don't die first." Making a weak stab at humor, Elizabeth walked out to the limo that seemed to instantly appear. For effect she closed her eyes and pretended to nestle into the back seat.

If she expected any pity from MacFarland, she had a long wait before her. He appeared to be focused on his own disappointment.

"See that you don't," he told her brusquely. "You owe me an evening."

She knew he wasn't talking about the pleasure of her company. In his opinion, he had paid for her entertainment via his art collection and he meant to collect one way or another.

It was enough to make her really ill.

"Yes," she murmured as he shut the door. "I know."

A shower, she thought as the car pulled away from the main house. She needed a shower. Badly.

Chapter 10

The light from the foyer pooled out onto the front walk. Cole was standing in the doorway, waiting for her when MacFarland's limousine pulled up. He didn't bother with an aloof facade. The second the vehicle stopped, Cole was beside it, opening the rear door and helping her out. With one curt nod at the chauffeur, he dismissed the man.

Slipping an arm around Elizabeth's shoulders, he ushered her into the house and closed the door.

"Are you all right?" he demanded, angry with himself for allowing this whole scenario to play out. Angry with her for making him care this much.

She bloomed before his eyes like a flower with its first taste of sweet water after a drought. All traces of the green-around-the-gills woman was gone.

Straightening, Elizabeth stared at him incredulously. "How did you get here ahead of me?"

"Never mind about that." Normally calm in any crisis, this scrambling and running in all directions at once sensation inside Cole was new and entirely unwelcome. He didn't know what to do first—carry her to her room or take her back outside to his car. "Do you need to go to the hospital?"

She laughed lightly, abandoning the shelter of his arms more reluctantly than she was happy about. It was getting late and she was tired. She began heading for her room. "Facing MacFarland wasn't that bad, although on a scale of one to ten—"

Grabbing her by the shoulder, Cole swung her around to face him. What the hell was going on here? Half an hour ago, she'd sounded as if she was at death's door. "Aren't you sick?"

"Well, figuratively speaking—"

"I mean physically, damn it. Back there, at MacFarland's house, you made it sound as if—" His own key words penetrated. *Made it sound.* Cole felt like an idiot. "It was an act, wasn't it?"

"Pretty convincing if I do say so myself." Elizabeth grinned and made her way up the stairs.

He knew his annoyance was way out of proportion, but he couldn't seem to harness it, couldn't seem to make it go away. All sorts of things had gone through his head on the drive back. "Yeah. You might have warned me."

She stopped by her door and looked at him quizzically. Everything had gone well. Why did he sound so irritated? "Why? Have you got a doctor on call, waiting to whisk me off to surgery?"

He realized that he disliked the high-handed way she spoke. And hated the fact that he felt so uptight, so shaken when he thought of her at that bastard's mercy. But then, he was beginning to get the feeling that Elizabeth would never be at anyone's mercy.

"No, but—"

Opening the door, she turned around to face him. "I didn't know I was going to do it myself until I saw those beefy lips of his coming straight at me."

The image was enough to make him shudder. Restraint kept him from doing it. "He didn't—"

She shook her head. "No, he didn't. But it was touch and go there for a few minutes." Pulling the pins out of her hair, she placed them on the bureau. "I'm sure that if he hadn't heard me throwing up, he might not have been so willing to let me go home."

He watched, mesmerized, as her hair floated down about her shoulders. The urge to lose his fingers in the feel of velvet was strong.

"You threw up." Then she really was sick, Cole thought.

"No, but he *thinks* I did." She combed her fingers through her hair. "Illusion is everything. He thought I was sick, heard the right sounds. That's all it took to convince him that having sex with me tonight might not be the smartest thing he'd ever do."

He blew out a breath. He should have thought this through. It just wasn't worth the risk. "And going over there alone might not have been the smartest thing you'd ever done.''

''Why?'' Her brows narrowed. Was he going to get all Neanderthal on her the way Anthony always did? ''I got the cameras planted. Now all we need to do is get them hooked up into the main cameras in his own system and we've got a bird's-eye view of the entire place.''

Try as he might, Cole couldn't get past the thought that he'd left her open to physical harm for his own benefit. ''You know, he might not have bought into that act of yours.''

Now she was getting annoyed. Why wasn't he letting go of this? ''The man is germophobic. He did.''

''But he might not have,'' Cole insisted.

How could she be so calm about it? Didn't she comprehend the consequences if something had gone wrong? Sure he was out there in his car, listening to every word. But what if he couldn't have gotten to her in time? His own ego had blinded him to that. ''Damn it, Gypsy, can't you get it through your thick head that he could have easily raped you?''

Easily? Hands on hips, Elizabeth jutted her chin out as she enunciated every word slowly. ''He could have tried.''

Damn it, why was she being so stubborn? MacFarland was a large man, as wide as he was big. And she was this delicate little thing. Bravado only went so far. ''And how would you have stopped him?''

She took off her earrings and left them on the bureau beside the pins. "In so many ways I don't want to waste my time talking about it."

Big talk, Cole thought. Maybe what she needed was someone to make her see that she wasn't the superwoman she thought she was. He moved so that he blocked her next move. "Show me."

Elizabeth cocked her head, trying to comprehend why he was behaving this way. She would have thought he'd be happy and be done with it. Why were men so difficult?

"Why?" she asked him.

"C'mon, show me," he urged in the voice of a disbeliever. "Show me what you would have done if he'd tried to take you against your will."

Even before he finished egging her on, Cole had grabbed her roughly, still angered by what he had almost allowed to happen.

The anger quickly left him as, less than a heartbeat later, he found himself flat on the ground, his arm twisted in an unnatural position, shooting slashes of pain up through the very roots of his hair.

Holding his arm captive, her heel at his throat, Elizabeth bent down until her face hovered over his. There was a smug look there that he would have given his soul to erase.

"Exhibit A," she told him complacently. Letting his arm go, she stepped back, keeping him in her line of vision.

Cole was quick to get to his feet. "I didn't see that coming."

Her eyes met his. "Neither would he."

He lunged at her then, just to bring his point home. The quick movement managed to catch her between his body and the wall. Elizabeth sighed, wilting just a little as if in surrender, and he knew he'd been right in being concerned.

The next moment, as their positions were somehow almost magically reversed and his arm was being jacked halfway up his back, Cole realized that maybe, just maybe, his concern might have been misspent.

Her face was less than an inch away from his. She let the moment sink in before releasing his arm. "Would you like me to continue? Or have you seen enough examples for one night?"

Cole rubbed his arm, working the circulation back through the limb. Okay, so maybe his fears about her safety were groundless. "Who taught you that?"

"The man I work for." Jeremy had been adamant about her ability to defend herself in all situations. He was that way about everyone who worked for him. "Or more accurately, he had someone teach me." Exhilarated and more turned on than she thought possible, given the situation, she took in a long breath and then released it. "He makes sure all his people are properly prepared for any eventuality."

His people. The phrase echoed in his head. Was she part of some kind of organization? "So there's more like you."

He wasn't asking, she realized, he was drawing a conclusion. "We are each individuals," she informed him. "Something else he taught me." Elizabeth deliberately kept referring to Jeremy by pronoun rather than by name. To the world, Jeremy was a man who took in desperate kids. Only the small band who were housed there knew what actually went on. And even when the times were rough and they might chafe to get out, loyalty to Jeremy was never a subject for question. It was a given, like the air they breathed.

Straightening his clothing, Cole found himself less than a breath away from her. The perimeter of the room was fading away.

The immediate circle around them tightened.

"So, how does one get the drop on you?"

"One doesn't." She could feel her heart begin to accelerate. Elizabeth raised her eyes to his. "Unless I want one to."

"I see."

They, or rather he, Cole silently amended, had just gone through a hell of a rousing example of foreplay. Without looking, he pushed the door closed. Then, crossing to her, he tilted her head back with the crook of his finger against her chin.

"Should I brace myself?" he wanted to know, his mouth close to hers.

Her heart was making the journey up to her throat. She needed to answer before she couldn't make a sound. "Oh, I'd say definitely."

He felt her smile against his lips a second before they were sealed to hers.

Everything he'd been feeling this very long evening, sitting in his car, listening for sounds, waiting to leap into action if she needed him, shot to the surface, bubbled over the top and then exploded.

Even before the kiss deepened, Cole was wrapping his arms around her, holding her close to him, knowing that tonight there was going to be no holding back. He couldn't. The ropes were far too frayed and the seals were all warped and broken.

The kiss grew in intensity, dragging him down to its core. Lighting him on fire.

It felt as if he'd held himself in check a thousand years. He felt that pent up inside, that volatile. That explosive.

She made him want to race, to feast on her as if she were a banquet that would be over all too quickly, whisked out of his reach like some impossible dream.

Or like Brigadoon rising out of the mists, to exist only for a little while before retreating back into shadows of another world not seen, to remain there for the next hundred years.

He needed to take all he could, to absorb all he could, before he woke from this dream.

A sense of urgency swept over him, coupled with an eagerness to touch her, to feel her before it all disappeared. Before his common sense stepped up to the plate to stop him.

He wanted her with a mind-numbing desire that brought him to his knees and made him afraid. Afraid to continue because this was a side of him he'd never seen before, and he didn't know where it would take him. More afraid to stop because he didn't know if he could stand the feeling of deprivation if he did.

He continued. The choice really wasn't his. It had

been made for him way before he'd ever gotten to this point.

Lips still slanting over hers, Cole felt along her back for a zipper. He felt like a man in a blindfold, searching for his way.

There was no zipper.

He felt her laugh bubble up against his mouth. And then she silently raised one arm. She took his hand and pressed it to her side.

Flesh met metal.

It was a strange place for a zipper, but he wasn't in any frame of mind to discuss location or what the designer had been thinking. He just wanted the zipper undone. Wanted Elizabeth's dress to be on the floor. Along with the rest of what she was wearing.

He took to his task with relish.

So this was it, she thought. This was what it was like to be on fire, finally on fire with desire, with anticipation.

With expectations.

Every inch of her, outside and in, was throbbing wildly. As he slowly slid her dress off her shoulders, letting it fall to the floor, she all but ripped his shirt from him. The beat of her heart echoing every movement, she quickly went to work on getting rid of his slacks. Her palms slid along his thighs as she dragged down his underwear along with the trousers.

Warm, seeking, openmouthed kisses commemorated every movement, every shred of fabric as it left their bodies. Excitement reached a fever pitch within her.

The room was spinning as he slid her panties off, then sealed his hands along the tender flesh of her buttocks, molding her to him.

Her breath, what was left of it, caught in her throat, lodging there.

She could feel the heat from his body searing her. Could feel his hard desire as it pressed against her, growing more demanding.

Suddenly she found herself tumbling backward, pressed against his hands as they cushioned her until she was against something soft. The bed. They were making love on the bed.

She'd envisioned a wide, luxurious bed when the first time happened. A suite in an outrageously expensive hotel. All those were fantasies for a young girl, she realized. Because it didn't matter where, it didn't matter when. All that really mattered was with whom.

And she had chosen this man. Chosen him from that very first moment in the gallery.

Their limbs tangled, breathing became audible, echoing in her head. She felt as if she was running toward something, reaching for something. And only being with him would get it for her.

The fire in her veins went up another notch.

She couldn't get enough of his mouth, would have been happy feasting on his lips the remainder of the night. But just as the thought whispered along her brain, she felt him moving elsewhere. He was kissing every single place he'd touched. Moistening it with his tongue, nipping at her with his teeth. Suckling until she was certain she'd lose her mind.

Twisting and turning her body, she tried to drink it all in. Sensations grew so demanding, the throbbing in her loins was so urgent, she bucked against him, not to move away but to have him sink deeper against her.

All of it. She wanted all of it.

Because this was her first time. And it was for all time.

Her hands slid along his body urgently, supplicating. She felt as if she was going to snap. Release, there had to be some sort of release. And yet, she wanted it to go on forever. She could die this way and it would be all right. As long as it was with him.

Cole couldn't hold himself back any longer.

Maybe with someone else, he might have been able to prolong the foreplay until she was reduced to some mindless puddle of undulating flesh, and then he would take her. But the trouble was, whether or not he was reducing her to anything at all, she had completely done him in. Made him her prisoner.

The soft whimpers, the eager movements, the sultry flesh that tasted of sin and temptation, all of it had undone him until he had no choice but to take her. Restraint was no longer part of the equation.

His mouth sealed to hers, he moved himself into position. Parting her legs with his own, Cole slid himself in, then stopped as something in a distant haze came to him.

There was resistance.

Not from her, and yet—

He opened his eyes and saw that she was watching him. Was that fear in her eyes? Or was it something else?

Second thoughts?

And then, before he could ask, before he could gather his thoughts in order to even form a question, she had wrapped her legs around his and raised her hips so that she rammed against him. There was a muffled squeal of pain and then she began to move. Move so that it stole every thought out of his head, everything but the need to join her in the last step.

He fell into rhythm with her, then took the lead until they were racing faster and faster to a summit he was well acquainted with.

He felt her nails digging into his back, raking over him as she arched and moved urgently. All thought stopped. He drove himself in further.

Finally the moment had come, and it was everything he knew it could be. Too soon it was over.

Paradise receded into the mists along the horizon, taking its unique brand of euphoria with it. Something else came in its place. An ominous feeling that he'd done something wrong, misread signs. Taken something precious that he had no right to.

Cole began to roll off her, then stopped. He felt Elizabeth's hands still pressed against his back, holding him where he was. Instead of rolling off, he pivoted himself on his elbows, raising up just enough to look at her.

A mass of confusion was running riot within him, as what he had done became clear to him.

"Gypsy?"

She heard it all in that one utterance, in that one name. Heard the questions, the confusion. Was that disappointment, too? She didn't want to think about that, only about how he'd made her feel.

As if she could touch the sky without ever leaving earth.

Before he could ask, she beat him to the punch. "You're my first."

Her first? That made absolutely no sense at all to him. They weren't living in the middle ages. Even then...

"How is that possible?" he asked.

"That you're my first? Because there's never been anyone else before you," she replied flippantly.

It had to be a lie, Cole thought. Yet, there'd been that initial resistance, and he knew pain when he encountered it and she'd made a noise that sounded very much like someone experiencing pain when she'd forced him to go further. Not that it had taken much doing on her part.

Rolling off her, he thought he saw what looked like uncertainty in her eyes. Cole gathered her into his arms. He kept coming back to the thought that it just didn't make any sense. "How can a woman who looks like you be a virgin?"

"It's called being selective."

"And you selected me?"

He wasn't sure just how to take that. He didn't

want to feel responsible, had spent his adult life trying to avoid just that because, being who he was, he never knew if women were drawn to him or to his wealth, his position. Having worked hard at building his empire, he wasn't about to lose it because of hormones. Not even to someone as unique as this woman.

"Let's just say we selected each other." She saw the wariness in his eyes and immediately reverted to her blasé, flippant persona, not wanting him to see just how much this had meant to her. "Don't worry, this doesn't mean that you're suddenly handcuffed to me. You're still free to work and play with others."

He didn't know if he liked the way she was just dismissing this, even though it made things a hell of a lot simpler for him. She'd all but blasted the foundations out of his world. Hadn't he affected her in kind? "That's not what I meant."

The wariness had left his eyes, replaced by something she couldn't begin to fathom. She only knew that it was melting down the steel fences she was trying to lock into place. "Then what did you mean?"

With each breath she took, she aroused him. He was having trouble thinking again. "How old are you?"

It was hard maintaining this facade around him when all she wanted was to kiss him, to have him kiss her. "Old enough to be lying here, nude, talking to you."

He needed to understand this, to make sense of it. And to figure out how he really felt about it. "You're what, twenty-six?"

Elizabeth smiled in response. Every woman liked looking younger than she was. "A little more."

"Okay, a little more than twenty-six," he echoed. Hell, he could have seen her being hit on in kindergarten by some cocky little five-year-old. "And in all that time, no guy's ever…"

"Oh, I wouldn't say that. They've 'evered.'" Elizabeth laughed, amused by the way his voice trailed off. Was that to spare her feelings? "They just didn't get anywhere."

He began to trail his fingertips along her throat. "Because you tossed them across the room?"

He was doing it again, making her crazy. Making her want him. "Didn't have to. I had a very protective brother."

He pressed a kiss to her earlobe. "And where is this very protective brother now?"

She was definitely having trouble thinking. "Don't worry, he's out of the protection business, at least as far as I'm concerned."

He kissed the point of her chin. "Does he know this?"

She found herself beginning to squirm again. Was this normal? Did it happen this way between a man and a woman, that they wanted each other more after it was over than before? "Afraid you're going to have to start sleeping with a gun at your side?"

He pulled her beneath him. "I'd rather start sleeping with you at my side."

He was flirting with her, she told herself, nothing more. He didn't mean anything by it. So she played along, fluttering her eyelashes at him. "Does this mean we're going steady?"

"It probably means I'm going straight to hell," he murmured, beginning to kiss her again as the heat, the desire, began to roar through his veins again.

She laughed, threading her arms around his neck. "At least you're already dressed for it."

Chapter 11

He'd had to endure three meetings in the morning and another in the afternoon, as well as quelling one potential crisis before he had a chance to be alone with his thoughts for more than half a minute.

Now, sitting in his office, Cole wasn't sure he wanted to be alone with them.

He'd never made love to a virgin before and, if he were honest with himself, he didn't quite know how he felt about the fact. Being first had never mattered to him. What counted, what had always counted, was being good. Being the best.

A hint of a smile curved his lips. In the absolute sense, he supposed that in this particular case it didn't really matter if he'd been at his best since Elizabeth had nothing to compare him to.

Best or not, he'd never felt so compelled before, so completely wrapped up in the act.

They'd made love once more that night, and he hadn't slipped out to his own room until well past the witching hour.

It seemed rather appropriate, seeing as how Elizabeth had completely bewitched him.

He sighed, threading his fingers together behind his head as he rocked in his chair. When he got right down to it, he still didn't know who she was.

As if some power higher than he was accustomed to dealing with was reading his mind, the door to his office opened less than a split second after a perfunctory knock. Hagen was in his office, closing the door behind him.

The man had obviously slipped by his secretary. Not an easy feat, Cole thought. Evangeline was going to be angry when she found out.

Hagen was holding a folder in his hands.

Dispensing with any polite chitchat or so much as a greeting beyond a nod, his chief investigator dove into the heart of the matter. "Finally got a clue."

Surprised to see him, Cole said nothing. The private investigator, who hardly ever garnered a second glance on the street, seemed to be dwarfed by his office, Cole thought. Short, balding, with an average face that tended to fade from memory before it ever properly registered, Hagen was good at his job precisely because he was so unmemorable. He wasn't one of those people who owned a room when they walked into it. He merely borrowed it on the sly, finding out what he needed to know before leaving again.

With something that might have passed for a flourish, Hagen placed the file on the massive desk, then turned it around so that Cole could read the name written across the top.

Cole raised his eyes to meet Hagen's. ''Elizabeth Payne?''

Hagen nodded, clearly pleased with the results of his efforts. ''It was changed to Caldwell, but it was originally Payne.''

Cole regarded the file, wondering what he would find there. Wondering what effect, if any, last night would have on the way he'd perceive the information. ''She changed it?''

Hagen made himself comfortable in the chair opposite his employer. He shook his head in response. ''Some social worker did it. She was trying to protect the kids from their old man.''

''Kids?''

Hagen's smile never seemed to be at home on his face. The features seemed to have been fashioned expressly to house a frown. ''Your lady is a triplet.''

Well, at least that much she'd told him was true, Cole thought. But he didn't care for the way Hagen had jumped to an assumption. ''She's not my lady, she's working for me.''

Hagen raised his hands as if to beg off giving offense. ''Sorry.''

Cole eyed the file. It wasn't very thick. But then,

it didn't have to be. He hadn't asked for chapter and verse, only the highlights. "What about the father?"

Hagen lifted his shoulders, then let them fall. That was still a loose end in his book. "Benedict Payne. Well-to-do family. Genius. Screw-up, always in trouble with the law. He disappeared. Nobody knows where. But all signs point to his offing his old lady before he skipped out."

Cole didn't particularly care for the man's cavalier references and apparent irreverence. He seemed not to take any note of the fact that these were people he was talking about, not just words on a page. "Any reason behind the killing, or was it just mindless domestic violence that got out of hand?"

Unable to keep entirely still for more than a few seconds at a time, Hagen began to rock ever so slightly in the chair. "Best guess is that she wouldn't tell him where she hid the kids."

Had Elizabeth's mother kidnapped her and her siblings to keep their father from getting at them? Or was there something more to this? "You mean the triplets."

Hagen inclined his head. It was obvious that he enjoyed doling out information a little at a time. "One of the sets."

Cole looked at him sharply. What the hell was he talking about? "One of the sets?"

The balding man nodded. He'd gone to a lot of trouble, questioned a lot of people to get at the information that was in the report.

"Rumor had it that there were more kids, another

set of triplets, but they disappeared soon after they were born. Maybe the mother killed them, I dunno. Maybe they never existed, but something definitely turned the old man into a loony tune.'' As he warmed to his subject, Hagen's mouth quirked in a grimace of a smile. He went into a terse summary of the rest of the events. ''Mother was buried, an APB went out on the old man, but they never found him. Kids went into the system, got passed around, ran away a few times, then ran away for good at thirteen.''

Elizabeth was thirty-one now. ''What about the eighteen years in between?''

The expression on Hagen's face gave no inkling of his thoughts. ''Nothing yet.''

Cole thought of the tidbit that Elizabeth had given him. The half smile on his lips had little humor behind it. ''No convents, huh?''

The two small, brown caterpillars that formed Hagen's eyebrows came together to mate over his nondescript nose. ''What?''

But Cole was already waving away the words. ''Never mind. Inside joke.'' Well, that certainly cast a different light on the woman who'd invaded and twisted her way into his world. She wasn't the carefree creature she tried to make herself out to be. ''Thanks, you did well.''

Though on his feet now, Hagen wasn't ready to go. There was something else, something more important, to tend to. ''What about that other matter?''

Cole knew Hagen didn't like being kept out of the loop, but right now things were under control. There was no need to bring him in again. Yet. "Venus is being taken care of."

Hagen allowed an impatient sound to escape his lips. "Yeah, but I should—"

Cole was quick to cut him off. "Let me do the worrying about that."

He liked Hagen, respected his talents, but he didn't like anyone making assumptions or trying to assume control when it came to matters that concerned him. He made the decisions, he issued the orders. Suggestions were accepted when asked for, not before.

With a reluctant nod of his head, Hagen began to take his leave.

"And, Hagen," Cole called after him.

The investigator paused at the door, waiting and clearly not completely content with his subservient role. "Yeah?"

Cole indicated the folder that was on his desk. "Nice work."

"Thanks." Hagen shut the door behind him. His expression hadn't been the kind worn by a man who'd just been complimented on his work.

Alone, Cole continued to sit there, silently contemplating the file on his desk. He hesitated to open it just in case Hagen had held something back. He'd already suspected that the lily-white story Elizabeth had given him was a lie. Nobody learned the skills she had at a convent, unless it was the kind of nunnery to which Hamlet had hotly banished Ophelia.

Still, he couldn't help wondering about the state of mind of a woman who had apparently lived through what she had. Was he dealing with one sharp lady, a potential liability? A possible threat?

And why the hell was there no record of her and her siblings for eighteen years? She didn't look like someone who had spent almost two decades in a cave of some sort.

It wasn't until the second ring that he realized the phone was ringing. With an annoyed sound, he yanked up the receiver. Now what?

"Williams."

"We have liftoff."

The sound of Elizabeth's voice in his ear, bright, pleased, brought all his dark thoughts to a grinding halt. And set off an entire collection of new ones. Bits and pieces of last night flashed through his mind, warming him. It took effort to bank them.

"And by that you mean…" Cole deliberately allowed his voice to trail off.

"Operation camera is a success," she informed him. There was no missing the smugness in her voice. "And you might like to know that I was right."

She could only be referring to one thing. But he needed to hear it. "You mean—"

"Yes." There was a pregnant pause for effect. She was enjoying this immensely. "In the sub-basement, along with other 'goodies.'" Elizabeth knew better than to mention the statue by name. You never knew when someone could be listening in. Nothing was a hundred percent safe.

Not even a man's arms, something whispered in her brain. *Especially a man's arms,* she told herself.

But she lacked conviction. Last night was still far too vivid for her to jadedly discount, even though she knew she should.

This was almost too good to be true. Cole had learned at a young age to be very, very skeptical. "You're sure?"

"Yes, I'm sure. I'd stake my life on it."

The happiness in her voice was seductive. Hell, breathing, when it involved her, was seductive, Cole thought. He needed to get himself under control. There were far more important things going on here than just the state of his suddenly overactive hormones.

"You won't have to," he told her. "I'll be right over."

Not waiting for a response, Cole disconnected the call, then put one in to his secretary. The remainder of his appointments for the afternoon needed to be rescheduled.

He bent a few speeding rules and availed himself of a shortcut as well. Excitement was his passenger as he took the less-than-scenic route back to his estate.

Standing over Elizabeth's shoulder a little more than an hour later, Cole stared at the screen. He couldn't help wondering how many times she'd done this before. Was she just a common thief?

No, he amended. There was nothing common about Elizabeth. At the very least, she was extraordinary.

But was she a thief?

For now he tabled the internal debate. As long as he kept his eye on her, things would turn out all right, Cole promised himself. He hadn't been born yesterday.

Just maybe reborn.

He looked back on the scene. The devices she had planted in MacFarland's mansion last night had been successfully linked up to the billionaire's main surveillance system, giving them access to every single camera on the premises. Cole was only interested in one of them. The one that was placed deep within the bowels of the mansion, in the sub-basement, in a room where MacFarland liked to keep his private, secret collection, viewed only by an invitation that was subject to the whim of the owner.

''That son of a—'' He bit off a curse. There was no point in giving way to anger. Pulling the switch back was going to be the sweetest revenge he could ask for. Trouble was, this was not going to be easy no matter how gifted the woman at the computer was.

Cole's hand was on her shoulder. Elizabeth doubted that he was even aware of it. But she was. Acutely so. It linked her not just to him, but to last night, which had very possibly been the best night of her life, although she sincerely hoped not. She hoped it was just one of a string of such nights, such encounters. That the best was yet to be.

Maybe because it had been her first time and maybe because she'd waited so long, she could have sworn the earth moved when they made love. She knew she wanted it to move again.

Shaking off her thoughts, Elizabeth glanced over her shoulder at him. "Is this the part where I get to say, 'I told you so'?"

Cole laughed, moving the chair around and tilting it back so he could kiss her soundly. "Yes, this is the part."

She blew out her breath. He'd done it again, knocked the pins right out from under her and stolen what there was of her air supply. "I'm going to have to catch my breath first."

He smiled into her eyes, the statue momentarily forgotten. "I can wait."

She swung her chair completely around to face him. If she wasn't careful, she was going to be swept away by her emotions. She needed to get down to business, if only to prove to herself that she could.

"I also think I'm right about how it happened. It's got to be an inside job." She saw the doubt creep across his forehead and didn't give him an opportunity to argue the point. "According to your man, he saw the statue being put into the crate." She repeated what she'd already told him earlier. "Someone switched it so that the crate was empty when it got there."

The probability that she was right was increasing. But it wasn't anything he wanted to address right now. Time was growing short. They needed a plan and they needed it now. The trouble was, his thinking ran along the lines of corporate business, not theft. "Hagen followed the truck with his car. He said the driver got a flat and he helped him change the tire. He was around the other vehicle at all times.''

She shrugged. ''I suppose someone could have switched it then, while the driver kept him busy. Still…''

Cole knew what she was thinking. ''It had to have happened after the crate arrived.'' He frowned. ''I'll deal with that later.''

No, he needed to deal with it now, at least in part, she thought. ''Until then, you're vulnerable,'' she insisted. ''Unless you don't mention this to anyone.''

He wasn't sure what she was driving at. ''Mention what?''

She tapped the screen. The bronze goddess, bathed in seductive blue lights, smiled alluringly at them from her perch. ''That we've located the statue and that we're going to get it back.''

This wasn't a two-person job. Even he could see that. ''Then how are we—''

''Just the two of us,'' she said firmly. And then, chewing on her lower lip as she studied the statue, she amended her statement. ''Actually, I think we're going to need a third.''

He immediately thought of Hagen. The investigator was still his most trusted man, despite her aspersions. ''Oh?''

''Yes.'' She swung around to look at him again, feeling that same rush coming into her veins, the one that accompanied a new venture, one that had her walking on the edge of a tightrope. ''I think I've figured out how we're going to get Venus back onto her pedestal at your gallery where she belongs.''

He felt something tightening inside his gut. Damn, but she looked as vibrant as she had last night when he'd made love with her. Everything within him yearned to take her now.

What the hell was going on with him?

He was behaving like some kid who'd just discovered sex, not a thirty-two-year-old man who had gotten to the stage where sex had become merely a pleasant diversion.

''Go ahead,'' he coaxed patiently. ''I'm listening.''

She summed it all up in one neat little word. ''Catering.''

That was a bit too terse for extrapolation. ''Excuse me?''

Taking a breath, she launched into her idea. It felt a little like a plunge down an eighty-foot roller coaster. She loved this part. ''MacFarland's having the party catered. There'll be servers all over the place. There'll be carts coming and going. Some will be standing still, out of the way.'' She looked up at him innocently. ''One of the carts, with an appropriate cloth over it, might even be parked in front of an unused door that leads down to the sub-basement.''

And so the impossible becomes a little less so, he thought. He caught her up in a hug. ''I do like the way your mind works.''

Pleased with herself, Elizabeth executed a little curtsy. ''Thank you.''

They had a lot of work ahead of them. Granted,

they had the layout of the house, thanks to the draw-ings the architect had filed with the city, and she al-ready knew the security system because of her own brand of ingenuity, which he was beginning to realize he couldn't question, but this last detail had to be factored in.

Cole began to leave. "I'll find out who the caterer is—"

Elizabeth held up a hand, stopping him. "Already done. He's using Royce of Philadelphia. They're very pricey, but he likes the food."

Cole crossed his arms before him, admiration in his voice. "You *have* been busy this morning."

She pretended to look humble. "I felt particularly energized."

Cole crossed back to her. "Funny, I would have thought you'd be exhausted."

She grinned. A warmth slipped over her, making its umpteenth reappearance today. "Maybe next time."

Taking her hands in his, he drew her up to her feet. "About last night—"

Leeriness elbowed aside the warmth. She raised her chin slightly. Defensively. She couldn't help it; it was in her nature to brace for disappointments. Maybe a little of Anthony existed within her.

"Is this going to be followed with a speech? Be-cause I think I've already made it clear that you don't have to worry about me."

Her resistance should have made things easier for him. It was, after all, the ideal male situation. A beautiful woman who wanted nothing in return except a good time. But it seemed to have the reverse effect. Her resistance just succeeded in reeling him in.

He slipped his arms around her, holding her to him. "I'm not worried about you. I'm worried about me."

"Oh?"

He felt her relaxing against him. And the leeriness had left her eyes. "I'm having trouble getting you out of my head."

She knew she shouldn't allow herself to be drawn in this way, shouldn't allow his words to matter. This was just an interlude. For God's sake, you couldn't fall for the first man you made love with. Any sucker knew that.

Right?

So then why...

"I'm small," she murmured, turning her eyes up to his beguilingly. "There's room."

"Seriously—"

She fluttered her lashes at him, negating her words. "Seriously."

He laughed and brushed his lips against hers. Damn, but he could take her right here and not even blink. Except to enjoy it far more than he'd ever thought humanly possible.

"Who are you, Elizabeth?" He had a file, he had data. He hadn't a clue. Not really. Because the woman in his arms wasn't really the woman in that file.

If you knew me, you'd reject me, Elizabeth thought. She was the entertainment portion of his life, nothing more. He was too far removed from her world for her to have any serious hopes that they could ever get together.

"Think of me as opportunity," she said glibly. "An opportunity to get back at MacFarland."

She was far more than that and they both knew it. The problem was, only one of them knew what that entailed. "And what's in it for you?" he asked.

She cocked her head as if to study him. "Is that your clever way of reneging on the fee?"

"Is that all that's behind this? A fee?" He sincerely doubted it. There had to be more. But what? In the end, was he going to regret throwing his lot in with her?

She slipped out of his arms, uneasy at the scrutiny. "I have nothing against MacFarland, if that's what you mean. After Saturday, once we pull this off, I think I'd probably like a restraining order. This is just a job for me."

This hardly fell under anyone's definition of a "job." "Someday you're going to have to fill me in on your job description."

Elizabeth laughed. The sound was as compelling as a siren's song. As long as he remembered what ultimately happened to the sailors who'd been lured by those sirens, he'd be all right.

Unable to resist, Cole took her into his arms again.

"Wanted—Female, brilliant, witty," Elizabeth recited. And then mischief entered her eyes. "Can say 'look, Ma, no hands,' and mean it."

He laughed and kissed her, this time with a little of the feeling that was coursing through his veins.

"You really are something else, Gypsy. I just haven't figured out what yet."

And you're never going to, because I won't let you. "Sometimes, magic tricks are best left unexplained. Otherwise, the magic fades."

"I don't think any amount of explaining will ever make your magic fade."

She smiled then, not grinned, but smiled, and he felt it go straight into his gut, taking him prisoner. "That may be the nicest thing anyone's ever said to me."

The temptation to remain with her, to spend the afternoon wrapped up in her, was tremendous. But he had an empire to run and obligations to meet even as he stood here. With effort, he stepped away from her. And felt oddly bereft, as if he'd just lost an opportunity.

He crossed to the door. "Will I see you tonight?"

There were things she had to set in motion. And a caterer to see. They had a statue to steal. "Count on it."

The house was quiet. Too quiet. He'd once enjoyed the sounds of silence; now it meant that the house was empty. That the children he'd taken in, people in their own right now, were out, either doing his bidding or their own. The end result was the same. Loneliness.

Funny how old age brings that to you on a tarnished platter. That and a host of feelings that had never mattered when he was a young man.

Jeremy Solienti sighed. His priorities had changed. Not that he was going to allow the makeshift family of enterprising youths he'd assembled over the years ever to see that.

He'd summoned Anthony, leaving a message on his voice mail to come see him the moment he got in. So when the door to his study opened after a respectful knock, Jeremy placed the book he was reading on the coffee table and welcomed the sight of one of his favorite people. His blue eyes grew a little brighter.

The brooding youth reminded him a little of himself at that age.

"You asked to see me," Anthony began.

Jeremy nodded. "Yes, I did. I've heard some disturbing things—"

Anthony instantly honed in on the one topic that hadn't been far from his mind since the blowup with his sister and her reckless disappearance. The note she'd left telling him not to worry about her hardly covered it. "Elizabeth?"

Jeremy knew the concern that was there. Knew, too, the origins. There was nothing about any of the young people he took in that he didn't eventually know. But it was time to move on. Elizabeth had done the healthy thing, struck out to be her own person. She was of more use to him that way.

"Only in a roundabout way," Jeremy assured him. "I've heard that someone's been asking questions."

Helping himself to a decanter of aged Irish whiskey, Anthony poured two fingers' worth into a shot glass. "Questions? What kind of questions?"

The rumblings hadn't been terribly specific. "Questions about you, about your sisters."

Anthony jumped to the only conclusion he could, given the situation. "The police?"

Jeremy waved a dismissive hand. He'd never really been concerned about the police mentality. There wasn't a detective he couldn't outsmart, even half trying. "The cops around here couldn't find their faces if they were looking in the mirror. No, someone else."

Anthony took a chair across from his mentor. "Who?" he pressed.

"Don't have a name. At least, not yet." There was a promise in his tone. A promise that he would find out. "Someone, though, who wants to find out all about you and the girls."

"Just us?" That didn't make any sense. "Or everyone who works for you?"

"Just you." With a nod of his head, Jeremy indicated that Anthony pour him a shot as well. Anthony rose to his feet and got another glass. "I never asked you kids anything." There'd never been a need. His network was extensive. But not infallible. He accepted the shot glass from Anthony, his eyes pinning the younger man. "But I'm asking now. Is there anything I should know? Did you kill anyone?"

"Hell, no," Anthony spat, sitting down again. "Although I wanted to. That guy who tried to rape Liz."

"Right." He knew all about that incident, as well

as the fact that Anthony had witnessed his mother's death. "Anyone else?"

"My father if I ever find him."

A lot of anger in that boy, Jeremy thought. Anger that he was going to have to find a way to work out of his system. "Can you think of any reason someone's asking questions?"

Anthony shrugged broadly. "Case of mistaken identity's my guess." Throwing back the shot, he finished it and got to his feet. He still had a job to see to. "Don't worry about it," he advised.

But Anthony was frowning as he left the room.

Chapter 12

"You know, there really ought to be a law," Cole told her.

Elizabeth's eyes met his in the mirror. Cole was standing in her doorway.

About to leave the room, she'd doubled back to take one last critical look at herself in the full-length mirror, to make sure she looked her best. Obviously, from the tone of his voice, she did.

Elizabeth turned around and looked at the man who'd brought all this about. Anyway you sliced it, in jeans or a suit, Cole Williams was one fine figure of a man. But he looked exceptionally handsome tonight.

The kind of handsome that was guaranteed to melt the glue right out from under a woman's expensive set of acrylic nails.

He was wearing a black tuxedo, black tie and white shirt, and just the sight of him made her feel weak in the knees. No man had a right to look that good and still be real instead of some wild fantasy.

Because she was accustomed to pretending, she carried off the act that she was unaffected by his appearance with aplomb. "A law against what?"

He took a step into the room, not knowing whether he trusted himself to come in any farther—to be alone with her. Tonight was about preserving his reputation, about getting back a stolen statue; it wasn't supposed to be about wanting a woman so badly his teeth hurt.

The ache didn't abate.

"Against a woman looking that good in a dress."

Good was a completely inadequate adjective in this case. So was *sensational.* The shimmering aqua dress she was wearing came up high at her throat and had long, narrow sleeves that reached her wrists. Only when she turned away did it became apparent that the dress was entirely backless all the way down to her waist. There was only about eighteen inches worth of material from there to the hem, which brushed seductively against her mid-thigh with every step she took and clung to her hips when she was standing still.

MacFarland was going to eat his tongue, Cole thought. He could feel his blood pressure rising just envisioning the other man's reaction to her outfit. To her. Maybe there was some other way....

With her arms out to the side, emphasizing the parts that were bare, Elizabeth slowly turned 360 degrees for his inspection.

"This is for maximum movement," she told him when she faced him again.

It wasn't only MacFarland who was in danger of swallowing his own tongue, Cole thought. He was having trouble keeping his in place. In an effort to divert his mind, he glanced down at her feet. She was wearing matching aqua sandals with four-inch heels.

Cole shook his head. "And those? Are they for maximum movement, too?"

She heard the skepticism in his voice and grinned in response. "You'd be surprised what I can do in a pair of heels."

All sorts of things began to suggest themselves to him. Things that had no place in the present situation and had nothing to do with removing a statue from its hiding place.

"You'll have to show me after this is over."

After this is over. Did he mean tonight, Elizabeth thought, or was he saying that they had a future after today?

She banked down her thoughts before they could run off in directions that would only interfere with her concentration. Besides, it was just a throwaway line, she told herself. Nothing to wrap her hopes around, and she was an idiot if she did.

Still…

Still nothing. She had a job to do and a fee to earn.

"Deal," she murmured. "By the way," she informed him as she picked up a small clutch purse from the bureau, "you paid for this."

He wasn't sure what she meant. "You're adding it on to the list of expenses?"

She stopped before him. "No." As if plucking it right out of thin air, she waved her hand and produced a credit card, then handed it to him. Her grin was as wide as the card. "I believe this is yours."

He kept all his credit cards in his wallet. And that was never off his person, except when he was sleeping. He remembered seeing that very card yesterday, when he'd checked for a business card he'd acquired the day before. Surprised, Cole raised his eyes to her face. "How did you…"

The smile wasn't so much smug as complacent. "Did you know that they used to refer to a pickpocket as a cut-purse back in Shakespeare's time? It's considered one of the oldest professions, right after motherhood and that other one." Her eyes were dancing.

Replacing the card in his wallet, Cole shook his head. "So you have pedigree."

"In a manner of speaking."

She glanced back at the clock on the nightstand. It was time.

Just before getting dressed, she'd made sure that the security system within the grotto-like area in the sub-basement wasn't going to be a problem. She'd done it the old-fashioned way, via the computer rather than on the premises with one of her "gifts." Anthony was better at that than she was, but she could hold her own if need be. And she was better at engineering things through the computer. She'd used it to loop a visual of the room so that no one watching the monitor would see her entering or leaving.

But all the ends weren't tied yet.

"Who did you get to coordinate with us?" she asked as they left the room. Cole had been very secretive about the matter when she'd asked earlier, telling her only to leave it to him. The rest of their plan had been reviewed ad nauseam until she could do it in her sleep.

Frustrated by this minor power play, she tried to appease herself by remembering that he was, after all, the boss and thus was paying her for her expertise.

Of course, he wasn't going to be the one lifting the statue from its pedestal. But then, he wouldn't be paying her the sum she'd asked for if he was.

Cole debated telling her who the third party was, but he wasn't in the mood for an argument. Once they were there, she couldn't very well walk out on him.

He took Elizabeth's arm, ushering her to the garage. "Why don't we save that for when we get there?"

She knew how to read faces and voices. And his were telling her something she didn't like. "It's Hagen, isn't it?"

Cole opened the door leading into the garage. "He's the best I have."

Hadn't he been paying attention to her? Why had he hired her if he wasn't going to take what she said seriously? "Hagen was also the best you had when the statue turned up missing."

There was no arguing with that, but there was still

his gut instinct. The same instinct that had him trusting her had him trusting the man he'd had in his em-
ploy all this time.

"Hagen knows what's at stake." He held the car
door open for her. "Anything goes wrong this time
and he's the prime suspect. Even if you are right
about him, he's not stupid. He won't risk it."

She slid into the passenger seat. "Men risk a lot of
things if the price is right."

He didn't answer until he'd rounded the hood and
got in on the driver's side. "What about women?"

"Women, too," she answered offhandedly. The
question got under her skin. He turned on the igni-
tion. The garage door directly behind them opened
and he backed the silver sports car out. She'd always
felt that the direct path was the best. Turning in her
seat, she looked at Cole. "Why, are you having second thoughts about me?"

His second thoughts were having second thoughts.
It had gotten to a point where he felt as if he'd come
full circle, twice over. "Just asking."

No, he was doing more than asking, she knew. He
was doubting, and maybe in the absolute sense, she
couldn't blame him for it. But in the emotional sense,
she could and did. "Say the word and I'll walk
away."

She couldn't be serious, he thought. They were on
the road. She couldn't open the door and get out. Just
then, the light turned red and he was forced to stop.
Was she responsible for that? "From the fee?"

''From distrust.'' Taking advantage of the moment, she released her seat belt and started to open the door.

Cole grabbed her by the arm, holding her as he bore down on the accelerator again. ''Hold on, don't go off half-cocked.''

Angry, she redid her seat belt. But it didn't change the way she felt. ''Oh, I am fully cocked, Williams, and loaded for bear.''

''Then I'd better get out of the way of your barrel.'' He spared her a look before turning back to the road. There was just the slightest hint of emotion in his voice as he said, ''I trust you, Gypsy. Don't make me wrong.''

''Not a chance.'' But because he had hurt her, and because she wasn't a hundred percent certain that he was being honest with her now, Elizabeth added flippantly, ''After all, you are the man who signs the check.''

''And don't you forget it.''

Both hands on the wheel, he made a left turn at the next light. Was that all he was to her? Cole wondered. That was all he was to a lot of people, a walking dollar sign. With her, part of him had hoped it would be different.

But how could it be? The woman earned her living by her wits. She was an opportunist. With very little effort, he could see the tables being turned, and him her target instead of MacFarland.

There but for the grace of God…

No, he wasn't going to cloud his mind with that now, he thought. There was no quick resolution in the offing. What there *was* was a statue to return to its rightful place.

He continued to make his way to MacFarland's mansion.

There were a glut of cars queuing up for the valets that MacFarland had hired for the evening. There were so many vehicles of all sizes, shapes and colors that it was more than easy to lose sight of just one.

It was what Cole was counting on. With Elizabeth as his lookout, he carefully backed his silver sports car up until he found himself at the other end of the mansion. At the rear entrance.

Cole looked around until he found who he was looking for. "Hey," he called out to one of the servers for the benefit of anyone else who might be listening. "What's the shortest way to the front?"

The balding man waved him over to the side, out of the way, then leaned in over the passenger side.

"Best way is to go back the way you came and make a right," he answered. His eyes remaining on Cole, he stealthily accepted from Elizabeth what appeared to be a large loaf of French bread wrapped in butcher paper. His expression gave no indication that he was actually holding a statue instead of food.

Withdrawing from the car, Hagen melded in with the other servers who were rushing around, all involved in trying to deliver a perfect party for an exacting taskmaster.

Elizabeth sank back in her seat, watching Hagen disappear into the house. "I really hope you're right about him,'' she murmured as Cole pulled away again.

She had created just enough doubt to make him a little uneasy. ''Yeah,'' he agreed. ''And I really hope you're wrong.''

As he slowly retraced his path back to the front of the estate, Cole was aware that she had stopped talking. Was that her way of showing that she was annoyed he'd gone with his instincts and used Hagen as the inside man? Or was she just being petulant because he didn't treat everything she said as gospel?

''Gypsy?''

The line in front of him was going particularly slowly, despite the fact that there were at least seven valets in play at all times. Easing his foot onto the brake again, Cole turned to look at her.

And saw that she had gone deathly pale.

''Gypsy?'' She made no response. ''Elizabeth, what's the matter?''

The urgent note in his voice echoed within the deep abyss she'd descended into, cracking the walls and letting in the light. She struggled to pull herself together. Tiny beads of perspiration had formed on her forehead. The horror of what she'd seen inside her head hung over her like a shroud.

Elizabeth took a deep breath. Her pulse was far from steady. She wasn't a clairvoyant by any means, wasn't given to visions or even premonitions most of the time, but just for a moment, through her mind's eye, she'd had a very clear picture of Jeremy, on the floor while men stood over him. Strange men who meant to do him harm. *Were* doing him harm.

There was blood.

Cole pulled over to the side, out of the long, curling line of cars. Losing his place. But he was more concerned with Elizabeth than getting his car properly attended to.

He put his hand on her shoulder and she jumped. There was definitely something wrong. Was she afraid of going through with this? After what he'd seen that first evening at his gallery, he would have said she wasn't afraid of anything, but she was a far more complex creature than he'd first thought.

"Are you all right?" he whispered.

With effort, Elizabeth shook off the feeling of impending doom. She tried to force a smile to her lips, but was far from successful.

"Yes, why?"

He didn't like being shut out this way. There was obviously something wrong and he wanted to know what. "Because I didn't think that a human being could turn that shade of white and still be alive. Now tell me what's wrong."

It was far too complicated to begin to explain now. He knew nothing about Jeremy, nothing about who and what she actually was. This wasn't the time to go into it. She shrugged, looking straight ahead. "I just…had a bad feeling."

That wasn't good enough. "About tonight?" Cole pressed.

She realized that he thought she was talking about

what they were going to pull off. If she took the easy way out and said yes, she knew he would ply her with a dozen questions. "No, about...a friend. It's probably nothing."

Damn it, he wished he was sure she was leveling with him. But he wasn't. The woman was a huge mass of secrets. "Look, if you're having second thoughts because I'm using Hagen—"

"Not the smartest thing you've done," she told him glibly, getting her wind back, "but we'll manage. Like you said, if this gets tripped up, then we know he's our man."

Elizabeth forced a smile to her lips, hoping her response would placate Cole. Wishing she could find a way to placate herself.

She couldn't shake the feeling that she'd just had a premonition.

They got back into line. Taking advantage of the lull, she closed her eyes and concentrated.

Anthony, if you can hear me, if you can sense me, find Jeremy. Find Jeremy, she repeated over and over, hoping that Anthony wasn't still blocking her thoughts the way he had been when she'd first moved out. *Please, Anthony, please let me in. Jeremy needs help.*

Anthony stared at the disks on his coffee table. Getting in and out of the lab had been so incredibly easy, it was almost insulting to someone of his talents. All he'd had to do was disarm the system, which was far from state-of-the art. His "gifts" had taken care of that.

The whole venture had lasted less than an hour from start to finish once he'd acquainted himself with the layout of the place. His sense of distrust coupled with intense curiosity had him making copies of the disks for himself. He intended to examine them when he got the chance, just to see what the fuss was all about. If he ran into trouble, he could always hand them over to Lizzie. She was a whiz when it came to software—

He stopped abruptly. No, no handing it to Lizzie. No Lizzie at all. Damn it, where had she gotten to? Why wasn't she—

Anthony stiffened. It felt as if a current had just zapped through him.

Was it his imagination?

Memories of communications came flooding back to him. When they'd been separated as children, he and Dani and Lizzie had communicated with one another like this in a desperate attempt to remain linked.

He shook off the feeling. Had to be his imagination. Elizabeth wouldn't try to get in contact with him. She was off somewhere, spreading her damn wings and pretending that she knew how to glide without colliding into buildings or whatever.

And yet…

And yet there was this urgency that was ricocheting through his brain. A feeling he couldn't come to terms with. It was like a message coming across with interference riddled all through it.

Something about Jeremy. About going to see Jeremy.

But he'd just been at Jeremy's house the other night. He was planning on going there tomorrow to drop off the disks for their client and get his share of the fee.

The urgency grew.

He couldn't rid himself of the feeling that if he didn't go now, it would be too late. He knew better than to ignore his instincts.

Anthony slipped the disks into an envelope, then placed the envelope inside his jacket pocket. Muttering a ripe oath under his breath, he got into his car and drove for the house he still considered his home.

"We know you know. Now, are you going to tell us where those freaks can be found, or do we have to beat it out of you?" The heavyset man with the shaven head whacked his fist against his palm. The sound thundered against Jeremy's ear.

"Why don't you make it easy on yourself, fella, and come clean?" his partner taunted.

The two men were both cast out of the same mold, bought for their muscle, not their brain power or their hearts. Between them, they hadn't enough for one, much less two. But they were good at their job, which was intimidation.

"You've already lost a lot of blood," the second one was saying. "No reason to lose your life."

Jeremy's eyes were almost swollen shut now, and his breathing was labored. They'd cracked two of his ribs, maybe more. He struggled to press his hand against the pain, but they'd broken his fingers and he couldn't.

His head was reeling. Part of him had always worried that he would come to this kind of end. What was it his mother had once said? *You lie with dogs, you're bound to get fleas.*

But this was a great deal more serious than an attack of fleas.

"Please." With effort, he managed to raise his hands before his beaten face, weakly attempting to ward off any further blows. "I don't know who you're talking about."

He wasn't a noble man, but this one thing, he could do. He could protect the three he had brought into his home. Most likely, it would be the last thing he would do.

Delirium was beginning to shred his thoughts. He struggled to hang on to consciousness a little while longer, terrified that once he let go, he would die.

"The trail ends here, you lying son of a bitch. You know," the larger of the two thugs insisted impatiently, his face a contoured mask of red. Swinging his hamlike fists back, he landed another blow on Jeremy's face, smashing his nose.

Suddenly, the door burst open.

The two thugs, both employed by Titan, found themselves looking down the barrel of a gun and a very angry man dressed all in black.

"You've got until the count of three to get the hell

away from him,'' Anthony growled at them malevolently.

One glance at Jeremy on the floor had his heart twisting inside his chest. Anger poured through Anthony's veins like molten lava. Even as he issued the ultimatum to the thugs, he was cocking the gun he'd taken from Jeremy's hall closet.

''You can't shoot both of us at the same time!'' the larger of the two thugs taunted. Momentarily abandoning their victim, the two men began to close in on Anthony.

''No, but I can kill one of you.'' Seething, barely able to restrain his desire to pump all the bullets in the handgun into the duo, he ground out the question, ''So, who's feeling lucky today?''

Handguns had never been his thing. Consequently, he wasn't much of a shot, but with a Magnum, he didn't need to be. Aiming it in the general vicinity of the target was all that was necessary to blow that target away.

And the two men knew it.

As if they were of one mind, the two men ran for the window. Glass broke as they dove right through, neither one of them wanting to risk being the one that Anthony chose as his first target.

At any other time, he would have taken care of business before they even reached the window. But right now his mind wasn't on killing, it was on saving. If he wasted time on the two thugs, it might be all the time that Jeremy had left on this earth.

It was no contest.

The two men were temporarily forgotten as Anthony dropped to his knees beside the man who'd pulled his sisters and him out of the gutter. Jeremy was bleeding badly and his breath came in short gasps.

"Who were they?" he whispered to Jeremy.

But Jeremy couldn't answer him. He'd slipped into unconsciousness.

For the first time in a very long while, Anthony felt tears gathering. Wiping his eyes with the back of his sleeve, he took out his cell phone.

"Hang in there, Jeremy," he ordered gruffly. "Help's coming."

He punched in 9-1-1.

And wondered where Elizabeth was.

Chapter 13

"Why don't you leave him?"

Elizabeth shifted her weight ever so slightly. MacFarland's arm was tucked possessively around her. It was as close to groping her as could be gotten away with in such a public gathering. She kept a seductive, inviting smile on her lips while doing a mental countdown. She had hoped to be in possession of the statue by now, but MacFarland had insisted on cornering her. He'd monopolized her for a good ten minutes now and gave no sign of letting up.

"Why?" She looked deeply into his watery eyes, imagining Cole's instead. "Are you going to make me an offer I can't refuse?"

"Perhaps." He ran his hand up and down her arm. It took effort for her not to shiver. "I know I could appreciate a woman like you far more than Williams can. Why don't you stay after the party and we can pick up where we left off the other night?''

"It's bad manners not to leave with the man who brought me.'' She paused significantly as a petulant expression came over MacFarland's features. "But there's nothing in the rules about not returning after I leave.''

He laughed then, looking pleased. The air of triumph in his manner threatened to turn her stomach. "I'll keep a light burning in the window.''

She ran her hand along his cheek, promise in her every gesture. "I'll look for it.''

Knowing that he was watching her, she turned and began to walk away, her hips a slow symphony of movement guaranteed to leave him wanting. Out of the corner of her eye, she could see Cole watching her as well. He didn't look like a man who was pleased by what he was witnessing. Was that for MacFarland's benefit? Or had an unguarded moment escaped?

She was allowing her feelings to color her perception. Of course it was for show. For Cole to be jealous, she would have had to mean something to him. She knew that. And yet…

MacFarland caught her arm. When she looked at him quizzically, he nodded in Cole's direction.

"He's watching us, you know.'' The edges of his smile became malevolent. "He looks jealous.''

She feigned interest as she studied him. "Does that matter?''

He made no pretense of indifference. She wouldn't

have believed it if he had. "Absolutely," MacFarland said with gusto.

You slime bucket, she thought as she smiled up into his eyes. Picking up a glass of champagne from a passing server's tray, she raised it before MacFarland. "To later," she toasted.

Holding her hand, he took a sip from her glass. "To later," he echoed.

"And now," she said, disengaging herself from the man, "I have to go make nice."

"Not too nice," MacFarland's voice followed her as she made her way toward Cole.

Elizabeth abandoned her drink on the first flat surface she encountered, not wanting to place her mouth anywhere near where MacFarland's had been. She was surprised her flesh hadn't crept off her body.

Glancing over her shoulder, she saw that her place had been immediately taken by several other people, all vying for the man's attention. Everyone wanted to get close to MacFarland.

Just as they did to Cole, she thought. It had to be hard, being a target for every hanger-on, every person hungry to advance. How did they ever go about separating the real from the fake? How did someone like Cole stay grounded?

Everyone had his problems, she supposed. Hers was keeping her mind on her work and not on the man who made her body temperature rise a few degrees every time she was close to him.

Their eyes met and she smiled, inclining her head

ever so slightly. Cole looked pleased. The hint of a smile on his lips made her heart flutter.

Damn it, she had to exercise better control over herself than that. But she couldn't wrap her head around the fact that this was only temporary. Her brain knew it, but somehow the message wasn't getting through to the rest of her. Where it counted.

Finally, she managed to reach Cole, much to the annoyance of the woman who was trying to monopolize his attention. He nodded toward the woman, then ushered Elizabeth to the side, away from the general crowd.

"So?"

She got in closer to him, making sure her voice didn't carry. "So he thinks you're jealous and he's all but jumping up and down with glee." It was the kind of behavior she just couldn't comprehend. "How could anyone as childish as MacFarland have gone so far in the business world?"

Because of the incident with the statue, he'd made it a point to become more familiar with the other man's dealings. In Cole's book, Jonathan MacFarland was only an average businessman, not a savvy one. "It helps to have Daddy's and Grandpa's money to play with. MacFarland's lost more than he's gained."

"Which is why he wants to get one up on you," Elizabeth concluded. She glanced at her watch. It was later than she liked. "I think I should get this show moving." Since he was in charge of this, she waited for his input. "What about you?"

"Sounds good to me." But as he began to go with her, Elizabeth shook her head.

"This is a one-person job," she whispered against his ear. "You can distract MacFarland if he comes looking for me. Feed his ego." They both knew that was the best way to go. "Tell him how well the show is going at the gallery. Let him dream a little about your upcoming fall from grace."

Cole grinned. "You are a wicked woman."

She laughed, patting his face. "You don't know the half of it."

But he wanted to, he thought, watching her disappear around the corner as she slipped behind the winding stairway. He really wanted to.

Making her way toward the rear of the house, Elizabeth saw the demographics of the people populating the area change drastically. In the front of the house were the beautiful people, dressed to the teeth, exchanging witticisms, oblivious of the "help" except when it came to having their glasses refilled. In the rear of the house were the working people. The servers, the caterers. All the ones who made sure the people in the front of the house had everything they needed to have a good time.

This was where Hagen was supposed to be.

She scanned the area, looking for him. She finally saw the man halfway across the kitchen, a tray of empty champagne glasses in his hand.

As if sensing her, Hagen turned his head in her direction. Eye contact was brief, accompanied by a slight nod. It told her everything she wanted to know. The cart, with the statue hidden on the shelf behind the tablecloth, was in place.

Keeping well out of everyone's way, Elizabeth made her way beyond the kitchen, toward the door she knew led down to the sub-basement—where MacFarland kept his rare treasures.

The cart, displaying a bright white linen tablecloth draped over it, was standing before the closet. Glancing around to make sure no one was watching her, she crossed to it and the door.

Just before she reached it, she disengaged the lock, making the door ready to be opened.

There was no one around. All the activity was in the kitchen and the dining area. Elizabeth raised the cloth and saw the package they'd given Hagen at the beginning of the evening.

Taking it, she quickly let herself in through the unlocked door and shut it behind her. There was just the barest hint of light inside the narrow passageway. It wafted like seductive smoke deep into the bowels of the mansion.

So far, no surprises, she thought.

Elizabeth paused to unwrap the package, removing the fake statue that Lorenzo had fashioned for Cole. Also packed inside were a pair of plastic gloves and the night goggles she used to see if there were any auxiliary laser beams still activated. Elizabeth slipped on both.

She'd already deactivated that part of the security system via the computer just before they'd left for the party, as well as threading a video loop so that she could go about her work unobserved by any cameras.

But she knew better than to take anything for granted.

Holding on to the banister, she made her way down the winding narrow stairs slowly. It felt as if it was taking forever, even though the distance from the top of the stairs to MacFarland's secret room was not that far.

Finally, she reached the room. Elizabeth paused before the door, concentrating. She took her time scanning the area, knowing that to hurry might cost her the entire mission.

But there was nothing.

No auxiliary system that turned on, no secondary alarms to deactivate. No silent alarms that went off when the slightest pressure was applied. It seemed that down here, in his private playground, Mac-Farland's ego took over. It was obvious that he felt no one could get by his men and his surveillance system on the upper floors. That made the room down here safe.

Hardly, she thought.

Just for good measure, she scanned everything again. The result was the same. All the safeguards had been taken out. She could proceed.

Acclimating to the room, Elizabeth walked in. Even if she hadn't been the art lover she was, the room would have taken her breath away. Under other circumstances, she would have loved nothing better than to sit here, drinking in the priceless works of art.

They made what graced the walls on the floors above pale in comparison.

The street price of what she was looking at was astounding. There were thieves she knew who would have killed to be standing where she was right now.

And then she saw it. Against the far wall, commanding attention and homage. *Venus. Smiling as if she had some sort of a secret to impart.*

Your only secret is that you are not *leaving with the man who brought you,* Elizabeth thought.

Inch by careful inch, she made her way slowly to the pedestal, taking care to scan her path every step of the way.

But again, there was nothing.

This was almost too convenient, Elizabeth thought. And when something was too good to be true, it usually wasn't true.

There had to be something she was missing.

And then it hit her. The pedestal that the statue was perched on was probably weight-sensitive. Which meant that the second she lifted the statue off, some kind of an alarm, some kind of signal, would go off somewhere, alerting a guard to what was happening here.

Elizabeth worked her lower lip. This, she thought as she looked at the statue in her arms, was going to take precision, a great deal of it.

Bracing herself, clearing her mind, she began to inch the statue slowly along the pedestal, bringing it to the edge at the same time that she moved the one she'd brought in to take its place. The process was slow, painstaking. Before long, her arms were trembling from the effort, not to mention the strain of holding one statue while balancing the other. They weren't too heavy, weighing in at approximately twenty-five pounds each, but they were swiftly approaching feeling like a ton each.

She could feel the perspiration forming at her brow, slipping along her breasts. The actual room temperature was cool—it had to be because of the paintings—but she felt as if she was standing in the middle of a sauna. She was sweating profusely.

And continued to until she finally mastered the switch an eternity later.

With a heartfelt sigh, Elizabeth placed the genuine statue on the floor beside her. Muscles were twitching all up and down her arms in silent complaint. She gave herself a minute to allow the rhythm of her heart to grow steady again, then she quickly wrapped up the statue in the butcher paper. Still wearing the goggles and the gloves, Elizabeth headed back up the stairs. She moved more quickly than she'd done going down.

At the top of the stairs, she stripped off her goggles and gloves, tucking them against the wrapped statue that she had pressed to her chest before she opened the door.

When she did, Elizabeth came to a full stop.

There was a burly guard directly in front of her, blocking her way. Her blood ran cold.

The man looked as huge as any lineman she'd ever seen charging on the football field and just about as friendly. He gestured toward the wrapped statue. "What've you got there?" he demanded.

"Roast beef," she answered without blinking an eye. "The caterer ran out. MacFarland asked me to get some from the basement."

"I'll bet," he growled. The guard reached inside his well-cut navy jacket. Whether it was for a gun or a walkie-talkie, she knew she was sunk. About to shove the cart into his gut and hope she was as fast in heels as she thought, she found she didn't have to be. The man crumbled right in front of her, hitting the floor with a thud that vibrated through to the soles of her feet.

Standing behind him, with an unopened bottle of champagne grasped by the neck, was Cole.

She breathed a sigh of relief as she checked on the guard's condition. Two fingers against his neck told her he still had a pulse, but he was clearly out.

She raised her eyes to Cole. "My hero."

He hadn't been content to just hang around while she put herself in the line of fire. There was no need for him to distract MacFarland. The man was doing a good enough job of that himself, talking to a group of people who seemed to be hanging on his every word. When Elizabeth didn't return as quickly as he felt she should have, the uneasiness Cole had been harboring all evening increased.

He went to see for himself if anything had gone wrong. And it had.

"We'll talk about that later." He moved back the tablecloth hanging over the cart, allowing her to deposit the statue safely onto the shelf. As a server, Hagen would transport the cart outside, leaving it where Cole could find it and reclaim the statue.

It was, he thought as Elizabeth had so glibly said, one big shell game.

Except for this extra large pea on the floor they had acquired. He looked at the unconscious guard. "How long do you think he'll stay out?"

He'd hit him rather hard, but the man had looked like a brick wall, able to withstand almost anything. "There's no telling," she answered. Elizabeth glanced around for something to use. "We need to tie him up and get him out of the way."

"Leave it to me."

Elizabeth turned around to see Hagen approaching. He produced a thin nylon cord from inside his server's jacket, then looked at her. He reacted to the expression on her face. "You can watch if you don't trust me."

"You know where to put that." Cole nodded at the cart. Taking Elizabeth's hand, he led her out of the area. "She trusts you."

She hurried to keep up. "No, I don't," she whispered against Cole's ear.

He didn't have time for this. "It was the shell game," Cole told her, having no other conclusion to reach. "They played musical crates after the statue was boxed up and Hagen signed off on it. He's innocent."

"You're sure of that." It was evident by her tone that she still wasn't.

Cole stopped for a moment. They were almost out in the open again, where the rest of the guests were mingling. "As sure as I am of you," he said softly.

She didn't like being lumped in with the likes of Taylor Hagen, but looking at it from Cole's point of view, she supposed it could have been worse. "And just how sure is that?"

"I'll let you know later."

They had the statue. In a few hours at the most, it would be back in his gallery, where it should have been all along. A rush began to overtake him. Giving in to impulse, Cole tilted her head back and kissed her quickly. The sensation went straight to his head, as he knew it would.

"We give Hagen ten minutes," he told her. "Then we leave."

"Before dinner?" Wanting nothing but to be gone from here, she pretended to shake her head in disapproval. "How rude."

"Before the security man is discovered," he whispered against her ear, creating warm waves that undulated over her.

"Good point."

Ten minutes never took so long.

Rather than make the rounds, Cole attempted to slip out quietly with Elizabeth. But just as they reached the front entrance, MacFarland came up behind them. "Oh, but you're not leaving already?"

They both turned to look at their host. "I'm afraid

so," Cole told him. "Elizabeth says she's not feeling very well."

MacFarland's eyes met hers. He seemed to be waiting for a confirmation of some sort from her that their earlier agreed-upon rendezvous was indeed on. "How dreadful. Nothing to do with the food, I trust."

"Just a little flare-up," Elizabeth replied. Then, to assure their getaway, she brushed a quick kiss along the man's cheek, whispering, "I'll be back," so that only he could hear.

MacFarland took her hand and raised it to his lips. He looked very contented with himself, she thought. The man was fairly beaming.

"I hope you recover very quickly." Releasing her hand, he nodded at Cole. "I'll see you when I come for my Venus."

"Yes, I expect you will." Cole slipped his arm around Elizabeth's shoulders and guided her out the door.

They were like two dogs, posturing, each claiming the same territory. Annoyed, Elizabeth shrugged off Cole's arm the moment they were outside the mansion. He looked at her quizzically.

"You did that for effect."

He had no idea why she suddenly sounded so irritated. "What?"

"Just now. You put your arm around me to annoy MacFarland." She blew out a breath. She knew it was all part of what she'd signed on for, but she didn't have to like it. Especially now that the parameters had changed. She didn't want to be just a pawn to Cole.

She wanted to be more. "Now I know what a bone feels like being tugged at by two hungry dogs."

He frowned at her. She'd known what they were doing. "Wasn't that the idea?"

"Yeah, it was," Elizabeth acknowledged tersely. That *had* been the idea. She had to remember that. Had to keep her feelings separate. *Easier said than done.*

Cole handed the valet his ticket. The young man went running off to fetch his car. "What did you say to him?"

Lost in thoughts she was trying not to have, she was caught off guard. "Who?"

Cole tried to read her expression and found that he couldn't. Probably all part of what she did, he thought. Casting spells over the unsuspecting. Because she sure as hell had cast one over him.

Or maybe that was the euphoria of being in the final stages of a plan well executed. He didn't know and didn't much care. The feeling was confusing enough. "MacFarland. Just now, inside, when you kissed him, what did you say to him?"

"That I'd be back."

No wonder the man had grinned like a loon as he'd watched them leave, Cole thought. In MacFarland's place he would have grinned, too. "Nice touch."

The valet returned with their car. Cole gave him a large tip that almost caused the young man's eyes to bug out. Elizabeth waited until they were both inside the vehicle before answering.

"Thanks." She snapped her seat belt into place.

"Now let's get out of here before they find the guard."

He was already making the turn out of the driveway. "Best idea I've heard all evening."

Appearing to take the road that led away from the mansion, he waited until he was out of sight of the entrance, then drove around to the rear. The cart, hidden by an expanse of tall shrubbery, was waiting just where he'd told Hagen to leave it.

"Just get close," Elizabeth told him. "You don't even have to stop the engine."

When he did as she instructed, she opened the door and leaned out of the vehicle. Securing the statue, she held it against her as she straightened again.

"Go, go, go," she cried.

He didn't even have to be told once.

The soft, small sound of pain had him turning from the window. Anthony had been looking out on the darkened parking lot, trying to gain some kind of perspective, trying to make sense out of the last few hours.

He was in the hospital, in the room to which the emergency-room doctor had assigned Jeremy. The older man hadn't regained consciousness the entire time. Not in the ambulance, not while the doctor and nurses worked over him in the E.R.

Anthony had almost climbed the walls after they'd taken Jeremy into the operating room. He wasn't much good at waiting. His patience had been all but frayed by the time the doctor had come out to see him, saying that Jeremy was going to be all right, but it was going to take time. The man needed to remain overnight to make sure nothing else would go wrong.

So they'd assigned Jeremy to a room and now he was here with his mentor, pacing off lengths, feeling as if he was going to go crazy. The situation confined him. He'd always hated confinements, hated being locked away.

He left the window and crossed back to Jeremy's bed. There was an IV rack in the way, tubes running into Jeremy to help sustain him. Anthony moved it to the side.

He saw that Jeremy's eyes were opened. For the first time since he'd met him, Jeremy looked old to him. Fragile.

Not the immortal force Anthony had always thought of the man as being.

Anthony took his hand, trying to will some of his energy into the thin frame.

Just like Dani and Lizzie had with Mom.

He angrily banished the thought from his mind.

The long, weak fingers closed around his. "You saved my life." Jeremy's voice was thin, raspy.

"Shh, don't talk," Anthony instructed. He could feel his throat closing up with emotion he refused to release. "The doctor wants you to rest."

But still Jeremy forced the words out. Words that needed to be said. "Thank you."

Anthony felt tears forming. Damn it, he wasn't going to break down. Couldn't break down.

"No," he contradicted. "Thank *you*."

It occurred to Anthony that he had never thanked the man for all the things Jeremy had done for his sisters and him. For giving them a life, an identity. For not making them feel like the freaks they might have been viewed as by an unaccepting world. Yes, he'd put them to work for him in time, but they had done that willingly, because they'd wanted to pay him back somehow.

"And I promise," he continued, "that I'm going to find out who did this to you and why."

Fear etched its way into the ashen face. "They want you, Anthony. I think they know about your…ability, and they want to use it somehow." He struggled for breath. "Be safe, boy," Jeremy begged.

Anthony smoothed the blanket around Jeremy, tucking him in. He shook his head, a sad smile playing along his lips. If it hadn't been for that strange sense of urgency that had channeled through him, he might not have gone to see Jeremy for several days. And Jeremy would have been killed.

"Sorry, old man," he told him solemnly. "Too late for that."

Chapter 14

"I believe the honor is yours."

Elizabeth presented the wrapped statue to Cole with a flourish.

Once more disconnecting the security system by use of conventional means, they had let themselves back into Cole's gallery.

Silence pervaded the room as only the paintings on the walls bore witness to what they were doing. In the center of the room, denuded of the blue beams which normally highlighted it, stood the empty pedestal waiting for the rightful statue to grace it, if only for the next twenty-four hours.

Tension whispered around them as Cole took the package Elizabeth had wrapped less than an hour ago and placed it on his desk. Until he saw it with his own eyes, he wasn't going to feel as if the venture was a success. Opening the desk's middle drawer, he took out a Swiss Army knife and sliced open the cords that were wound around the statue. He peeled the paper back. Bronze gleamed like warm flesh as it emerged.

To the untrained eye, it looked exactly like the statue that had been standing on the pedestal since the opening—the statue that was now residing within MacFarland's precious treasure room.

But it was the trained eye Cole knew he was going to have to reckon with once MacFarland came for his statue. When they had struck the deal, Jonathan MacFarland had insisted on bringing his appraiser with him when the exhibit ended. At the time, it had seemed like little enough to ask and Cole had readily agreed.

Now he understood the reason for the request. MacFarland meant to humiliate him, to bring his reputation into question publicly, in front of an audience.

His mouth curved. The best laid plans of mice and men…

Slipping the knife back into the drawer, Cole raised his eyes to look at Elizabeth. And waited.

She looked at the statue very closely. She took her time. It amazed Elizabeth how well preserved it had remained over the years. But then, the statue appeared to have received nothing but loving care in all that time. Art was priceless, timeless, a way of declaring to the world that something beyond barbarians walked the earth. She felt honored just to be in the same room with it. In a way, she could almost understand

MacFarland's possessiveness. But that was only self-ishness speaking. Above all, art had to be shared, not hoarded.

"Well?" Cole pressed when he couldn't hold back any longer.

She blew out a breath, relieved. "It's not a copy." She'd been half afraid that another switch had been made, that Hagen had been the inside man despite Cole's faith in him and that he'd made off with the original.

"No," intoned another voice in the room. "It's the original. And thanks for getting it for me."

They both turned in unison to see Hagen walking in through the back entrance. Not thinking beyond the moment, Cole hadn't reactivated the alarm system. They were only going to be here long enough to place the statue on its pedestal and then leave.

Still wearing the caterer's short gold jacket and black slacks, Hagen appeared to have followed them from the estate.

The man moved into the room slowly, like a tiger stalking its prey. Toying with it. There was a gun in his hand and a glint in his eye that Elizabeth was all too familiar with.

It was the look of a man who didn't care if he added another kill to his résumé.

Damn it, she'd been right all along, she thought. She'd never taken less pleasure in the fact.

Cole moved protectively in front of Elizabeth. "Hagen, what do you think you're doing?"

Hagen's tone was condescending. "Becoming my

own boss.'' His eyes darted over toward the statue and then back at the two people in the room. His lips peeled back in a cold smile. ''Not that you weren't a good one to work for, but you see, I'm tired of taking orders, tired of watching someone else make money.'' He spared another possessive glance at the statue. It was apparent by his behavior that he could care less about art. It was the money that interested him. ''MacFarland's going to pay plenty to get this baby back.''

''So you're double-crossing him, too?'' Elizabeth asked. It seemed par for the course to her.

Hagen bristled at the contempt he heard in her voice. She was no better than he was. Worse. ''Man's gotta look out for himself.'' The cold grin broadened. ''You should have listened to her when she told you not to trust me. Glad you didn't.''

''Why did you do it?'' Cole demanded.

''Why does anyone do anything? Money. Mac-Farland offered me more money than I could walk away from.'' All pretense at civility vanished as his eyes darkened. ''Now wrap that up for me, sweetheart, and make it snappy.'' He nodded toward the paper that had just been removed from the statue.

Elizabeth remained where she was. ''You're going to kill us.'' It wasn't a guess.

The bone-chilling smile was back with an extra dose of malevolence. ''Like the pirates used to say, dead men tell no tales.''

Her hands still raised, she looked at Hagen with

complete contempt. "You want it wrapped? Then do it yourself."

Enraged, Hagen shifted his gun so that it pointed at Cole. "Want to see him get it first, bitch? You asked for it." He began to squeeze the trigger, but it wouldn't budge beneath his finger. He pressed harder. It still remained frozen in place. "What the—"

Cole glanced at Elizabeth. One look at her eyes told him what she was up to.

Elizabeth never took her eyes off the investigator. "It won't move," she informed Hagen calmly.

A string of curses polluted the air. Hagen's frustrated anger was all that Cole needed. He dove for the man, knocking him to the floor. The inert firearm went flying out of reach.

The fight was short and over quickly. Without the benefit of weapons, when faced with rage, Hagen found himself at a disadvantage. He had only the statue to gain. Cole had that and a great deal more. He fought as if his life was on the line, which it was. More importantly, Elizabeth's life was on the line.

Finally backing away from the unconscious man, Cole shook his right hand, trying to temper the sting he felt across his knuckles. They always made it look so easy in the movies, he thought.

He continued looking at Hagen, watching for any signs of a return to consciousness. Cole rubbed his knuckles with his other hand. "Nice to know my time in the gym wasn't misspent."

Despite the danger, Elizabeth had discovered that the physicality had excited her. She was beginning to suspect that watching Cole shelling peas would have excited her. "You keep this up, you can go into a whole new line of work. Cole Williams, mercenary."

"Retired," he added. As far as excitement went, he preferred his between the sheets—with her. Crossing over to where Hagen's weapon had fallen, Cole used his handkerchief and picked up the gun. He examined it, just lightly touching the trigger. There appeared to be nothing wrong with it.

He looked over toward Elizabeth. "You do something to this, Gypsy?"

She was bending over Hagen, checking the pulse in his throat. The man was very much alive, just knocked out.

"I might have temporarily frozen the metal in place. Why?"

He laughed, shaking his head. The woman was at least part witch. Maybe more than just part. "You're one of a kind, Gypsy."

No, she thought, rising to her feet, she wasn't. But now wasn't the time to tell him what Dani had recently told her. That there were more people like them. More people who could do extraordinary things. No, that kind of a bombshell was for another time.

If there was going to be another time, she amended. But she and Cole had had enough excitement for the night.

She looked at the unconscious man on the floor. "What do you want to do with him?"

Cole's personal code of trust had been violated. He

wasn't so naive as to think that just because he'd trusted someone, they were blameless, but this was going to take a bit of adjusting to.

Was he wrong to trust her, he wondered.

Was he ever going to be rid of that feeling of uncertainty?

"That's for the police to decide," Cole finally told her.

She thought of Hagen's part in the switch. And of what he might know about her. After all, he was an investigator. Wouldn't it stand to reason that he might investigate someone he didn't care for in order to get them out of the way?

"What if he talks?" she asked.

Cole had already considered that. "What's he going to say? That he was paid by MacFarland to steal the original before it reached my gallery? That he was coming to take the original back in order to ransom it back to MacFarland?" His eyes met hers. "After all, we've got the whole thing on tape."

He'd surprised her. So, he'd caught on to that, too, had he? "You disabled the security system," she pointed out innocently.

He'd begun to anticipate the way her mind worked. "And you turned the camera back on when he turned up at the gallery." Taking his cell phone out, Cole was pressing 9-1-1 on his keypad. He nodded at the camera that had been placed over the doorway to his office. "I saw the red recording light go on." Anticipating her or not, she still managed to astound him. "You know, you really are an extraordinary woman."

Extra-ordinary, she thought. It could be taken so many ways. "You don't know the half of it," she laughed, using the same phrase she'd used earlier.

His response was still the same, except that this time he said it out loud. "No, but I intend to," he promised before turning away from her.

The dispatch had come on the line.

Elizabeth felt as if she was riding on the highest cloud in the sky the entire trip back to his house. It had taken the better part of two hours to get everything moving in the proper direction. Hagen had been arrested for attempted robbery and attempted murder. She had no doubt that Cole's former chief investigator would try to plea bargain his way out of a lengthy jail sentence by offering up MacFarland and his part in it.

From what she'd managed to glean in a short time, MacFarland's dealings did not bear up to close scrutiny. It looked as if Cole was going to be short one hell of a thorn in his side.

"I guess he won't be here with his appraiser tomorrow when the statue is crated up to send back," Elizabeth commented as she allowed Cole to help her out of the car. Tension danced through her body. It was an entirely different kind of tension than the one she'd experienced earlier this evening. This one had Cole's name written all over it.

Make love with me one more time, Cole.

"Too bad," he mused. He unlocked the door and they walked in. "I was kind of looking forward to seeing the look on MacFarland's face when the appraiser told him that the statue was real.''

Taking off her shawl, she dropped it over the banister. ''Maybe if you know someone in the police department, you can be there when they come to arrest him for fraud and whatever else Hagen has to offer up about him. That expression should be priceless.''

Yes, he thought, it should be. Almost as priceless as her expression was when they made love. ''MacFarland's not clean.''

She grinned. ''Not like you,'' she agreed, running her fingers through his hair. Missing him already. ''I like a clean man.''

He locked his arms around her, as if to keep her from escaping. As if he could. ''Tell me more.''

''Uh-uh.'' She wiggled out of his grasp, but didn't move away too far. ''A girl's gotta have her secrets. Otherwise the mystery's gone.''

He laughed dryly. ''If you ask me, you've got more than enough secrets. The mystery about you, Gypsy, is never going to be gone.''

He was making it sound as if it wasn't over, she thought. As if they had a world of tomorrows before them. But that was just wishful thinking on her part. And wishful thinking didn't make it so.

What she had, she knew, was tonight, and she was going to make the most of it.

Moving back toward him, she wrapped her arms around Cole. ''You do know how to turn a girl's head,'' she murmured, turning her face up to his.

She seemed to fit so perfectly against him. "It's not your head I'm interested in right now."

"Oh?"

"Not that I don't appreciate a smart woman," he qualified, lightly combing his fingers through her hair. "But there's been something I've been dying to do all evening."

She could feel it again, that quick heating of her blood, that racing of her pulse. There was nothing like it. "And that is?"

"This."

Cole placed his hands on her shoulders and slowly moved the shimmery material down along her arms. It fell away from her flesh with a sigh, which in no way compared to the one of contentment that escaped his lips when he looked at her.

She was nude to the waist.

He had a feeling that if he moved the fabric down along her hips, he would discover that she wasn't wearing anything at all beneath her dress.

The very thought had him growing harder, wanting her. She'd been in his bed every night from the first time they made love, but each time had left him wanting more, living both in the moment and in the anticipation of the next time. Because each time seemed to be better than the last. And not as good as the next.

How was that possible?

His brain swimming, he wasn't up to untangling the philosophy. All he wanted to do was separate her from the shimmering cloth and bring her to him.

His hands spanned her waist, making her stomach

do flip-flops. She didn't understand it. She could remain utterly cool and calm in a life-and-death situation, such as the one she'd experienced tonight. Yet
the very touch of this man had her quaking inside,
desperate to mold her body to his.

Desperate to have him want her.

She drew her breath in as he moved the material
down away from her hips. Everything within her
tightened like a harp about to be strummed.

She heard him catch his breath. And loved the look
in his eyes as they slid over her body. Making her
burn for him.

"I see you didn't waste any money on underwear."

Her smile was beguiling and she knew it. "I didn't
want to max out your card."

He lost himself in the fragrance along the column
of her neck. She felt, as well as heard, his words.
"Very thoughtful of you."

She could feel her eyes drifting shut as pleasure
closed in around her. "I try."

And then Cole didn't want to talk anymore. Didn't
want to do anything but feel the taste of her lips, feel
the soft yielding of her body as he filled it.

He kissed her over and over again. Kissed her
throat, her face, her hair, the plain above her breasts.
He touched her everywhere, stroking, caressing. Pos-
sessing.

It wasn't enough. Cole began to doubt it ever
would be.

It was getting increasingly difficult to hang on to

her thoughts. ''Don't you think we should go up-stairs?'' The question came out in a rush.

''No, I gave the housekeeper the night off.''

And then there was no time to talk, no breath with which to say anything else. He stole it all away from her. Cole lost it himself. Lovemaking with her was far too taxing, far too consuming, to waste even the tiniest bit of energy on anything else.

Her head was spinning as he reduced her to a mind-less, pulsating mass of desires and needs.

There was just enough of her intuition left to let her know that she had done the same to him. Eliza-beth gloried in the triumph as something akin to a frenzy swooped over her.

She was barely aware of tearing away Cole's cloth-ing, of throwing herself into a full-body assault of him that involved every inch of her.

She touched, she caressed, she conquered, using her tongue, her teeth, her hands, the very skin along her body as she rubbed it against his. She was going to make him hers.

Or, at the very least, make him remember her for the rest of his days.

''Hold it, Gypsy,'' he gasped, wrapping his arms around her to stay the assault for a moment. ''This isn't a contest.''

She raised her head, her hair a swirling velvet cur-tain on either side of her face. Her green eyes danced as she looked at him.

''I know. For it to be a contest, you needed to have stood a fighting chance.''

He laughed as he sealed his mouth to hers.

And then he took her. Took her before he had no energy left with which to do it.

Her muffled cry against his mouth empowered him and he drove them both up to the place they'd craved from the first moment.

Anthony felt completely drained. Tired beyond any words. But he also felt relieved.

Jeremy was going to be all right.

The man's hold on life had proved to be a great deal more tenacious than it had first appeared. He was not about to go gently into that good night, Anthony thought cynically. But it was at a cost. Although, until yesterday, he'd thought of Jeremy as invincible, he couldn't think of him that way anymore.

It grieved him.

Whoever had done this to his teacher, his surrogate father, was going to pay. Even if he hadn't sworn that to Jeremy, he had to himself.

No one was going to harm anyone he cared about ever again.

He fumbled for his apartment key, his mind locked into the past. If he'd found a way to stop his father, his mother might have still been alive today. At the very least, she would have lived longer.

That thought haunted his nights, invaded his days. There was no way that he was about to allow anything like that to happen to Jeremy or his sisters. He couldn't live with the burden of that.

He should have killed the two thugs where they

stood; it wouldn't have been a difficult matter for him. He could do things like that. Destroy at will if he wanted to. And those two thugs had been less than vermin. He would have felt worse stepping on a spider.

But he'd been so worried about Jeremy, he hadn't been thinking straight. And the two men had escaped. To what end? Would they be back?

He made up his mind to find them before they found Jeremy again.

But he needed rest. Rest to recharge, to come up with a viable plan.

Finding his keys, he let himself into the apartment and reached for the light.

Someone grabbed him from behind.

An arm snaked around his throat, choking him just enough to immobilize him. He felt something hard being pressed into his spine.

A gun?

"Don't give me any trouble," the voice growled. The voice came from above him. Whoever this was, the person was taller than he was.

A blow to the head was coming next.

Anthony sensed it. Knew it. Whoever this was wanted him alive, not dead.

The next moment, he used his assailant's weight against him and threw the man to the floor. He'd wrenched the gun out of the man's hand, but the heel of the man's boot clipped him across the temple as he went down.

Dizzy from the blow, Anthony took a second to pull himself together.

It was all the time his attacker needed.

When Anthony finally threw on the light, he saw that he was alone. Whoever had attacked him was gone.

And with him, the reason for the attack.

All he had to go on was Jeremy's warning that someone was looking into his and his sisters' pasts.

Which meant that they all might be in danger.

Why?

There were no answers for him.

Frustrated, Anthony locked the door and went to tend to his wound.

Chapter 15

Cole turned his face toward hers. "I didn't know a person could be this exhausted and still be alive," he confessed.

They were in his bed together and he'd lost count of the number of times they'd made love through the night. True to form, each time had been better than the last, more rigorous than the last. It still astounded him. He wouldn't have thought that was possible. But with Elizabeth, all things seemed possible.

He smiled at her. "You wear me out, Gypsy."

"That's the general idea."

Her voice was hardly above a soft whisper. Even depleted of all energy, he found it incredibly seductive. He had no way of knowing she was speaking so softly because she had hardly any energy herself.

It was the middle of the night and darkness was

pervading all the corners of his room. He wanted to see her, just to look at her because he hadn't the strength to do anything else.

Turning from Elizabeth, he reached for the lamp by his bed, only to have it go on before his fingers brushed against the switch. He stared at the lamp for a moment, getting his bearings.

He glanced at her over his shoulder. "That was you?"

She laughed at the slight note of uncertainty in his voice. "That was me."

Cole shook his head as he turned back to Elizabeth. He slipped his arm around her and drew her close to him. The warmth of her skin whispered along his body.

"I don't think I'm ever going to get used to you doing that."

There he went again, phrasing his words so that it sounded as if he meant for the two of them to be together beyond the night.

Maybe he did, she thought. After all, there was no reason to end this just yet. They were both consenting adults, consenting to have a good time.

And that was all this could be construed as, she insisted. A good time. It couldn't be anything else to her because it wouldn't be anything else to him. Pretending otherwise was just that, pretending. She hadn't the power to make him fall in love with her, the way she knew she had fallen for him.

Even if she did, even if fate or nature had given her the ability to bend people's wills to her own, she wouldn't have done it. Because then she'd never know if Cole was with her because he wanted to be or because she wanted him to be.

She sighed, curling up against him, taking comfort in the feel of him against her. In a way, she supposed it wasn't unlike the situation that Cole was constantly in, wondering if people liked him for himself or for the money he had, the position he had.

He raised himself up on one elbow and brushed the hair back from her temple. She seemed to be a million miles away. "You look lost in thought, Gypsy."

Lost, that was a good word for it. That would be the way she'd feel once they went their separate ways. Lost. But right now she was here and so was he. And she'd always believed in making the very most of what she had.

"I am."

He pretended to glance around at all the surfaces in the room. "Anything moving?"

Mischief in her eyes, she grinned as she dipped her hand beneath the sheet and brushed her fingers along his thigh. "You tell me."

He caught his breath as he felt her fingers feathering along his body, touching him intimately. Making him respond. He could have sworn he was spent for the night. And here she was showing him that there was still more firepower left.

"Damn, but you are good." He laughed. "I think you could make a dead man want you."

"I'm not interested in a dead man," she murmured. Shifting, she brought her face next to his and lightly traced the outline of his lips with her tongue. "I'm interested in a man who's very much alive."

It was the last thing she said for a while. Because he'd stolen her breath away again.

Cole reached for her even before his eyes were opened. Reached but didn't find her.

Opening his eyes, he found that he was alone in his bed. A quick pass of his hand told him that the place beside him was cool. The scent of her body was just barely clinging to the sheets.

A sense of urgency shot through him with the speed of espresso coffee, jolting him completely awake. Rising quickly, he pulled on a pair of slacks he got from the closet and went looking for her.

The same sense of urgency had now ushered in a feeling of pending loss. He couldn't put his finger on the reason behind it, just knew it was there.

Maybe he'd been spending too much time with her.

No such animal, he told himself.

Cole hurried to her room. Reaching it, he didn't bother to knock. Instead, he threw open the door. Elizabeth was fully dressed. There was a suitcase on her bed. The one she'd brought with her when she'd first arrived. She was just flipping the locks closed as he entered.

He felt as if he was standing on the bridge of the *Titanic,* watching the iceberg approach. "What are you doing?"

Damn, she'd hoped to make her getaway before he woke up. She'd done a great deal of soul searching in the wee hours of the morning while he'd slept at her side. While she'd pretended that he would always sleep at her side.

Delusion, all of it.

Her common sense and feeling of self-preservation had waged one hell of a wrestling match with her feelings. She wanted nothing more than to stay, to be around so much that he couldn't imagine what life had been like before she'd entered it.

But she refused to be a beggar, even in theory. If he wanted her, he'd come for her, he'd tell her that he wanted her. And if he said nothing, if it didn't matter to him whether she stayed or went, well there was no reason to hang around like some pathetic soul invited to a party who had long overstayed her welcome.

"I'm getting ready to leave," she replied crisply. "As of last night, the job's over. We got the statue, we got the inside man responsible for the theft in the first place—" she ticked off the points on her raised fingers "—and, unless I miss my guess, after Hagen finishes making his deals with the D.A., you'll never have to worry about MacFarland again." She moved her hands as if ushering in a drumroll. "All with your reputation sparklingly intact."

She took a deep breath as she removed the suitcase from the bed and placed it on the floor beside her. "Everything you ever wanted."

Not everything, he thought.

Nerves began to dance through him the way they never did, no matter what deal was on the table. Still, she looked so calm about what she was saying. Didn't it matter to her? He wasn't about to put himself on the line if she could just walk away like this. A man had his pride. "Is this what you want?"

No, this isn't what I want. I want you to tell me you want me to stay. I want you to make love with me until I completely melt, like a bar of chocolate you've held in your hand too long.

She tossed her hair over her shoulder in that familiar way of hers, he noted. But her eyes remained distant, leaving him confused. "What I want or don't want doesn't have anything to do with it. This was the deal."

Last night he would have bet his vast empire and his immortal soul that they had made the kind of connections poets only dreamt about. But maybe he'd deluded himself. Maybe only he'd made that connection while she had just enjoyed herself.

The virgin's a fast learner, he thought bitterly.

Feeling a hole opening up within him, Cole shoved his hands into his pockets. In one pocket his fingers came in contact with a piece of paper.

And then he remembered.

"Well, in that case, here." He took out the folded piece of paper from his pocket and handed it to her.

Taking it, Elizabeth opened it to find that it was a check. Neatly signed by Cole. For a hundred thousand dollars more than the amount they'd first agreed on.

She had her own code of honor. She always had. She held the check out to him. "I can't take this. It's too much."

He made no attempt to take it back. "You've earned it."

She didn't like the sound of that. Her back stiffened as she bristled at the implication. "The nights were complimentary."

Cole's eyes narrowed. Did she actually think that he was about to demean the time they'd spent together? That he was putting a price on it and paying for her "services"?

He could feel himself getting angry. Was that what she thought of him? Of them?

Damn it, he hadn't a clue. He sincerely wished that she was easier to read.

"I was referring to the fact that you were right about Hagen. If I'd kept him on, who knows where this all might have led?"

"Right. Hagen." Since he wasn't taking it back, she looked down at the check a second time. No, there was no way she was going to take it. Deal or no deal, she'd changed her mind.

Grabbing his hand, she pressed the check into his palm. "Keep it," she growled at him.

Any insight he thought he'd possessed when it came to the female mind evaporated. He was clearly a novice here. But they'd had a deal, an arrangement.

"What? Why?"

Because I don't want your money. I want you and if I can't have you, I don't want your money, either. But he needed a plausible reason, so she gave it to him. "This was my first solo caper. It's on the house."

He saw something in her eyes. Something that broke through the barriers. Something that told him his initial take on this hadn't been wrong. He took heart. Folding the check until it was small enough to fit inside the space of her closed hand, he pressed it back on her. "But you have to take it."

This was getting ridiculous. She could refuse payment if she wanted to. "Why?" she demanded. "Why do I have to take it?"

He looked at her, the soul of innocence even as a hint of a smile began to break through. "Because then, how else am I going to marry you for your money?"

Completely dumbfounded, she could only stare at him. "What?"

He hadn't meant to say anything about marriage. The word had just slipped out. But now that it had, it felt right. The whole idea felt right. "I've got a reputation to uphold."

"Yes, I know. You're squeaky clean."

And hooking up with her, Elizabeth thought, would make him anything but that, even if she renounced any connections to Jeremy. Cole's world was a completely different one from hers, and if he had any idea whom he was actually dealing with, he'd be horrified. Better to leave now, before he found out.

She'd turned away from him. Cole moved so that he was in front of her again. Suddenly, he knew that he was fighting for the most important thing in his life. He couldn't afford to have her walk out on him. His world would never be the same.

"No, not that reputation. The one where I always make savvy acquisitions."

Her eyes narrowed. *Wait a second here.* "Is that what you think I am? An acquisition?" Her voice went up several octaves as she repeated the word.

Her mood didn't improve any when he laughed.

"I had a feeling you were going to take that the wrong way. Glad I can at least predict something about you." And then, before she could tell him to take a flying leap, he took her hands in his, becoming serious. "I had you investigated."

Her confidence slipped a notch. She would have sworn that he wouldn't be able to find out anything about her, but the way he looked at her told her that he had. What? What did that weasel Hagen tell him?

As always, when everything else failed, she brazened it out. "And?"

"And I don't care," he told her simply. "I don't care what you did before we met. All I know is that you're the most exciting woman I've ever come across." He grinned, for once able to read the thoughts that were crossing her mind. "Even without that knack of yours for making things float and move. The point is, Gypsy, I'm not about to let you get away."

Whether he knew it or not, he was still making her sound like a possession. Maybe that was his world, but it wasn't hers. She'd just declared her emancipation from Anthony; she wasn't about to slip her neck into another yoke.

There were ground rules to establish, and if she didn't do it now, she might never get the chance.

"Look, I'm not an object to hold on to or drop. It's not up to you whether or not I 'get away.' If I stay or go, it's because it's my choice, not yours—"

There was more. Maybe a lot more, but she didn't get a chance to say it, didn't get a chance to let her thoughts link up into one another, because Cole pulled her into his arms and kissed her.

Kissed her long and hard. The heat between them was so intense, she worried that she'd go up in flames.

Elizabeth anchored her fingers on his shoulders, holding on as she sank deep into the folds of his kiss. Letting her head spin.

Letting the room fade.

He took her soul and sent it on a whirling ride that left her wanting more. Her body temperature had soared and her brain felt feverish.

Taking a deep breath, Cole stopped kissing her. Because if he didn't, there would be no stopping. She made him hungry in so many different ways, it completely messed with his mind. And he needed her to resolve this, to tell him that she would stay. That building a life together wasn't out of the question for her.

She was a unique woman. Precisely because any other woman with her background would have jumped at the chance to join the truly legitimate world. Yet she hadn't said anything to make him feel as if he'd won his case.

Smiling into the green eyes he'd grown to love so well, Cole coaxed, "You were saying?"

She looked at him, dazed, just barely able to focus her eyes, but hardly her mind. "Was I talking?"

"Yes." He always made use of opportunity when it presented itself, giving credence to the old adage about all being fair in love and war—and this, he knew, was a little bit of both. "I believe it was something about agreeing to marry me."

Very slowly, as a smile bloomed on her lips, she shook her head. "I don't seem to remember that."

"Think hard." He brushed his crooked finger along her cheek. He was winning. He could feel it. "I definitely remember the words *marriage* and *yes* being uttered."

And then she laughed. "Liar."

"No one's ever accused me of lying," he told her, keeping a very straight face. "Because I don't."

"You and George Washington, right?"

He tucked his arms around her again. He had a good feeling about this. Things were definitely turning his way. "Man stole the cherry tree story from me. So, is it yes?"

She pretended still to be debating her answer, even as everything within her sang *Yes.* "You're rushing me, Williams."

"Sorry." He brushed a kiss to her temple, then lingered there a moment, allowing her sweetness to penetrate his senses. "How much time do you need to say yes?"

She leaned her head back to look up at him. "What makes you think I'll say yes?"

Well, there he had her, Cole thought. "You wouldn't have kissed me like that if no was on your mind."

"There's nothing on my mind," she told him in a moment of complete honesty, trying her best to look peeved. She failed. "You sucked it all out."

"I can do better." And then, because he knew he'd won, because he knew it was going to be all right, he said the words he realized hadn't been uttered yet. Words she needed to know as much as he needed to say them. For the first time. Forever. "I love you, Gypsy."

Melting, she was melting. Right here, right now. She sighed, thinking that she couldn't remember ever being happier. Not ever.

"You're right, you can do better." And then she looked at him, afraid to grab this happiness with both hands. Afraid of being disappointed again. She searched his eyes. "And you're sure about this? You want to marry me?"

He'd never been more sure of anything in his life. "I already told you, I don't lie."

She pretended to be serious. "That could be a problem down the road."

He drew her even closer, silently reveling in the feel of her. "Only if I join your line of work."

That was something she hadn't thought of. As his wife, she couldn't very well be sneaking into places, pulling off jobs. And yet, she didn't want him to order her to stop. It was a gift she wanted to offer him.

She studied his face. "Then you wouldn't tell me to give up my life?"

She was her own person. It was what had caught his attention from the very first. He'd no more try to subdue and change her than he'd geld a prize-winning thoroughbred. "How could I? It's what makes you be you."

"I'd be a liability."

Was she deliberately trying to make him tell her to leave her life? "Never happen."

The sigh that escaped her lips had *blissful* written all over it. Elizabeth threaded her arms around his neck. "You do love me, don't you?"

"That's what I've been trying to tell you." He paused, waiting. When she made no attempt to say anything, he prodded, "How about you?"

Her eyes were sparkling as she told him, "I love me, too."

"Gypsy—"

"And you." She laughed, and there was pure joy in the sound. "I love you, too." And then she shook her head, a sliver of concern pricking at her. "But you really don't know what you're getting into."

"So?" His shoulders rose and fell carelessly. "You've got the rest of your life to show me."

"There you go, ordering me around again."

Cole inclined his head obligingly. "I'll have to work on that."

"Don't," she cautioned. "It's what makes you be

you. Besides,'' she added mischievously. ''I like wrestling for the top position.''

He orchestrated his first negotiation. ''How about we split that, fifty-fifty? Half the time you can be on top, the other half I'll be on top?''

Her eyes shone. ''We're not talking about arguments, are we?''

''We're talking about anything you want to talk about. But we're talking about it later.'' Like a man with a mission, he began to undress her.

She could feel her body priming. Anticipation. A vague memory teased her brain. ''Don't you have an early-morning meeting?''

He wasn't about to leave this room until after he'd made love with her even if the president was calling an emergency meeting.

''I'm the boss.'' He threw her blouse aside, going to work on the skirt. ''They won't start without me.''

Tit for tat, she thought, as she unzipped his trousers. ''Just as long as you don't start without me,'' she whispered.

He could feel that by now familiar feeling tightening his gut, filling his loins. It was a feeling he was determined to continue being familiar with for the next half century or so. Maybe longer. You never knew about the advances science was going to make.

''Never happen,'' he promised just before his mouth came down on hers.

Epilogue

He could sense it.

Sense her happiness.

As Anthony sat alone in his small, utilitarian apartment, feelings came to him like warm waves of water in the dark.

For the first time in her life, Elizabeth was truly happy. It was an unshackled happiness, not hampered by doubts, by fears. Happiness in its purest sense.

Something he knew Danielle felt, too.

Something he knew he never would experience himself. Happiness was something that had eluded him, would continue to elude him. He couldn't recall a single instant when that unfettered sensation had soared through him. The closest he'd come was to have burdens lifted from his shoulders. By Jeremy.

Jeremy who was doing better this morning. Jeremy who needed to be avenged.

Probably the man who'd tried to kidnap him early this morning was somehow connected to the men who had beaten Jeremy so badly.

But who?

Why?

He was going to have to find out the answers himself. He knew that he couldn't rely on Elizabeth's help anymore. She'd crossed over, gone to the other side. The side where normal people resided.

In simple terms, she'd abandoned him. Just as everyone else had.

Anthony felt lonelier than he ever had in his life.

But there was no time to spend pitying himself. He had a job to do. He had to find out who had tried to kill Jeremy and who was asking all those questions about his sisters and about him.

And he was going to have to do it alone.

* * * * *

Look for the next exciting installment in
FAMILY SECRETS:
THE NEXT GENERATION
when
TRIPLE DARE
by Candace Irvin hits the stands.
Coming in August 2004.
Available wherever Silhouette Books are sold.

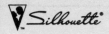

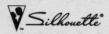

A NEW MILLENNIUM, A NEW ERA, A NEW KIND OF HEROINE.

She's a strong, sexy, savvy woman who is just as comfortable wearing a black cocktail dress as she is brandishing blue steel.

Look for the new and exciting series from Silhouette Books featuring modern bombshells who save the day and ultimately *get their man!*

Silhouette Bombshell™ launches July 2004 at a retail outlet near you.

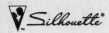

COMING NEXT MONTH

INTIMATE MOMENTS

#1309 IN THE DARK—Heather Graham
Alexandra McCord's life was unraveling. The body she'd discovered
had disappeared—and now she was trapped on an island with a
hurricane roaring in and someone threatening her life. To make
matters worse, the only man she could rely on was the ex-husband
she'd never forgotten, David Denhem, who might be her savior—
or a killer.

#1310 SHOTGUN HONEYMOON—Terese Ramin
No one had to force Janina Galvez to marry Native American cop
Russ Levoie. She'd loved him since his rookie days, but their lives
had gone in separate directions. Now his proposal—and protection—
seemed like the answer to her prayers. But would he be able to save
her from the threat from her past, or would danger overwhelm them
both?

#1311 TRIPLE DARE—Candace Irvin
Family Secrets: The Next Generation
Wealthy recluse Darian Sabura had resigned himself to a solitary
existence—until he heard violinist Abigail Pembroke's music. Then
Abby witnessed a murder, and suddenly it was up to Darian to keep
her alive. But would she feel protected—or panicked—when she
learned he was empathetic and could literally sense every private
thought?

#1312 HEIR TO DANGER—Valerie Parv
Code of the Outback
The Australian outback was about as far as Princess Shara Najran of
Q'aresh could go to escape her evil ex-fiancé. With her life at stake,
she sought sanctuary in the arms of rugged ranger Tom McCullough.
But when her past loomed, threatening Tom's life, would Shara run
again to protect the man she loved—or stay and fight for their future?

#1313 BULLETPROOF HEARTS—Brenda Harlen
When D.A. Natalie Vaughn stumbled onto a murder scene, Lieutenant
Dylan Creighton knew the sexy prosecutor had just placed herself on
a crime kingpin's hit list. And when they were forced to work
together to bring him down, their powerful attraction for each other
became too irresistible to deny.

#1314 GUARDING LAURA—Susan Vaughan
When it came to guarding Laura Rossiter, government operative
Cole Stratton preferred jungle combat to a forced reunion with his old
flame. But having someone else protect her from a madman
determined to see her dead wasn't an option. Would Cole's nerves
of steel see him through the toughest battle of his life—winning
Laura's heart?

SIMCNM0704